HELEN HARVEY

EMMY LEVELS UP

OXFORD

UNIVERSITY PRESS

LEVEL:
NEWBIE

ONE

As Emmentine chants, the statue of power begins to glow. Swirling runes carved into the statue burn bright white. Sizzling tendrils of magic shoot from the rock. Emmentine opens her fanged mouth wide and swallows them down like fiery spaghetti.

```
Status: Magic bar full
```

She's ready to face the Mulch Queen.

My fingers tap on the keyboard and Emmentine bounds up the mountainside with catlike grace, into the gaping maw of the cave.

```
Checkpoint: Entering the
Putrid Caverns
```

In the darkness, ghostly orbs flicker awake, lighting a maze of stalagmites that grasp like witches' fingers at Emmentine's boots. She zigzags this way and that. One more bend, one more leap, and there it is: the green fog.

I knew from the first time I saw it that this fog was dangerous, but I'm not scared any more. Emmentine has beaten every Mulchbeast and now there's nothing left to do but face the Mulch Queen and win.

She charges into the fog and suddenly she's falling. As the tunnel walls fly past, my fingers are poised. I go over the plan in my head one more time…

Boom, Emmentine lands on the cavern floor, and *rumble*, everything shakes as a shapeless mouldering pile erupts, *poof*, into a four-armed monster. The creature rises to fill the cavern, her skin like slime, her dress made of thorns and rotting leaves.

The Mulch Queen has awoken!

Emmentine is already running as *slam*, a boulder-like fist smacks the floor behind her. Emmentine swipes with a burning claw, tearing three fiery gashes in the Mulch Queen's side. She casts Dazzling Lights and pellets of fire spew from

2

her palms. The Mulch Queen wails and flails her arms as flames punch through her skin.

She belches out a cloud of poison gas, but Emmentine dodges as I hammer out the key combo. A Cone of Repulsing Flame flies from Emmentine's mouth. Layers of the Mulch Queen rip off in ashy flakes. She shrinks to a ball of brambles as her health drops to almost zero.

```
Bind the Mulch Queen before she
gains too much health
```

I know exactly what to do.

Around the cavern are four spell crystals, each resting in an alcove in the glittering wall—if I can rearrange the crystals, the curse will turn on its maker.

I have to be quick.

Emmentine runs to the purple crystal. *Flash,* she snatches it in one magma paw. She runs, *flash,* swaps it for the red crystal. Coloured light swirls and vines snake about like they're searching for something.

Run, *flash,* the light swirls faster, the vines waft higher, but the Mulch Queen is shaking now, she's nearly recharged. Run, *flash*. The lights are spinning too fast, the vines waving too wildly.

'Put the crystally thing in the flashy thing!' says Ryan behind me.

I jump. 'I know!' I didn't hear Ryan get home. And there's only seconds left.

The Mulch Queen roars. One more crystal, one more flash, and *whoosh!*

The vines snap around the Mulch Queen like a closing fist.

Wailing and writhing, the captured Mulch Queen sinks into the cave floor.

The cave roof cracks open and sunlight pours in. The festering mulch shrinks away. Flowers and trees sprout from the rock, but I'm barely watching now.

I stand up so fast my chair tips backwards into Ryan's stomach. I wave my stripy blanket like a flag as I leap around the living room.

'I did it! I did it! I defeated the Mulch Queen without taking any damage. Yes, yes, yes!'

'Why are you jumping, Emmy?' Ryan takes the desk chair. 'It wasn't that hard.'

'You don't understand, I think I just did a world record or something. I bound the Mulch Queen and she's the final boss on Illusory Isles, and I did it in record time, and Emmentine kept full health the whole way through. And I videoed the whole thing for my gaming channel, and, and, and, WOOHOO!' I jump and skip and leap on the sofa and nearly trip on a cushion and land, *bang*, beside Ryan, my socks skidding on the laminate floor.

'You couldn't do it,' I tell him. 'Not even IndigoChalice could pull off a binding like that. MeowMeow thought it was impossible, but I tried and I tried and I finally did it.'

'Who are InvisibleCabbage and MooMoo?' says Ryan, clicking on NEW GAME. 'Seriously, these people have the weirdest names.'

'It's IndigoChalice and MeowMeow, and they are my two best friends on the Illusory Isles message board. Obviously.'

'You're just friends online though, right?' says Ryan as the CHARACTER BUILDER screen loads, and my stomach goes tight. 'Not real-life friends?' I try to shove him off the chair with my shoulder, but he's too heavy.

'Online friends *are* real friends.'

'What's "The Way of the Bottle"?' he says, reading off the screen. Ryan has this trick of changing the subject just when I'm really annoyed at him. It works though.

'That means you play as an enchanter and do magic using potions,' I tell him, trying not to show that he's bothered me. Not showing you're bothered is part of the rules for little sisters. 'My character isn't an enchanter though, she's a fire elemental. Elementals can do magic with just their hands and voices. They also look way cooler. Emmentine looks like a lion.' I jump onto the sofa arm behind him. 'See, you don't even know how to play. As if I needed your help.'

'You were about to tank before I came along,' Ryan says, colouring his character's hair bright pink, then sunset orange, then pitch black. 'How do I fight that slimy woman?'

'She's called the Mulch Queen.'

'Oh, the *Mulch Queen*,' he says, not very seriously. He always talks like this with me, like everything is a big joke. Probably from being a teenager.

'She's trying to take over the Illusory Isles with her evil mulch.'

'Oh, the *mulch*,' he nods, wisely. 'So how do I fight her?'

'You can't, not yet. She's the final boss, and she's really hard to beat.' I bounce up and down on the sagging sofa arm. 'But I just did! Even though I know she isn't completely beaten because Illusory Isles II is coming out in less than a week, and everyone is saying that the Mulch Queen comes back, and I can't wait!'

The front door scrapes open.

'Hi, kiddos!' says Paul. There's a clattering noise and a big bang like something heavy crashing into the wall.

'The tattoos for the fayre are here,' Mum shouts.

'What are you up to?' Paul sticks his bald head round the living room door. 'That game again?' He winks.

'Come and see these tattoos!' Mum shouts from down the hall.

'I was actually just showing Emmy how to defeat the Munch Queen,' says Ryan.

'*Mulch Queen*,' I correct him. 'And I bound her myself actually. Do you want to see?'

When Paul comes over, Ryan jumps up from his seat, pulling at his school tie. Ryan gets like that with Paul sometimes.

I replay the video of the fight and Paul makes

impressed sounds in all the right places. When the
vines snap around the Mulch Queen, Paul punches
the air.

'Nice one, Emmy! I bet you're excited to show
your friends at school,' says Paul.

But suddenly I'm knotted up. 'No one at school
really plays Illusory Isles. No one I know, anyway.'
I try to imagine what Vanessa or Ria would say if
I showed them the video. Lila might think it was
cool, as long as Vanessa and Ria weren't around…

'You should,' says Paul, grinning like he doesn't
know he's said anything wrong. 'Have you been
playing too, Ryan?'

'Just showing Emmy what to do.' He shrugs.
'It's not really my thing. Babyish.' At that I feel
even more knotted up. I thought Ryan was getting
into it.

'I know full-grown men who play Illusory Isles,'
Paul protests.

Mum appears in the doorway. Her purple hair
has gone extra frizzy, which makes her look like
a witch. My hair does the same thing, but it just
makes me look messy.

'Are you lot coming to see these tattoos or not?'

In the kitchen, a huge cardboard box is open on

the table. It's full of temporary tattoos: dragons, kittens, football logos. Mum is a real tattooist, with a shop and everything, but every year for the summer fayre at school she runs the face painting and temporary tattoo stall.

I try not to think about school, but the idea spreads in my brain like mulch slime.

'I knew they'd arrive in time.' Mum nudges Paul. 'Scaremongerer. You said they wouldn't be here for months and months.'

'I don't think scaremongerer is a word,' Paul says. He's been Mum's boyfriend for two years now and moved in soon after Christmas.

'Shall I sort the designs out?' asks Ryan, picking up a sheet of rainbow unicorns.

'No, I want to sort them,' says Mum, plunging her tattooed arms into the box. 'That's the best bit.'

'Guess I'm making dinner again,' says Paul.

'Emmy, could you print a sign with the prices on it, like last year?' Mum asks.

'I could test the tattoos,' Ryan says. 'Check they're not gummy, like two years ago.'

'Oh yeah, and get yourself a freebie,' says Mum.

'No, I just thought we don't want another gummy year.'

'Haven't you got homework to do?' Mum runs her hands through her hair so it sticks up even more.

'What? I'm just trying to help.'

Paul sets a pan on the cooker. 'Leave it, Kiddo. Looks like you can just chill out.'

Ryan huffs as he leaves the room.

I print out the price list for Mum. Then I edit my video and upload it on Islandr, the Illusory Isles message board. MeowMeow and IndigoChalice will drop dead in amazement when they see it. No one has defeated the Mulch Queen without taking any damage before. No one but me.

Islandr Message Boards

Video: Binding the Mulch Queen – NO DAMAGE!!!

play video

29 views · 7 likes

Emmentine

I bound the Mulch Queen without taking a single hit.
WOOHOOOOOOOOOO!!!!!!!

Comments

MeowMeow
OMG YOU DID IT! YOU LEGGEEEEEEEND!

IndigoChalice
Right this is on. I'm gonna bind her with zero damage in even
less time. Battle of the mulch, sista!

TWO

'Today we're writing an adventure story,' says Miss Monday the next day in English. Miss Monday wears big glasses that make her look like she's glaring. I always think she's about to tell me off, even though I haven't done anything wrong. 'I'm looking for quests and dragons and magic, not forgetting best handwriting.'

Handwriting is my worst thing.

I shoot a look at Vanessa, who's sat on my table since she joined Springhill Primary School just after Christmas. She's pale and freckled and tall. Her strawberry blonde hair hangs like a curtain over her book as she starts her story.

I scribble the title in my exercise book and start writing as fast as I can. I'm not a good writer, but I'm very quick and when I've written a page and a half Miss Monday will let me stop.

As usual, Marcus's hand shoots up straight

away. Marcus has brown skin and curly hair that's always getting in his eyes because he's trying to grow it long.

'Have you got me my laptop yet?'

Marcus's parents took him to a specialist, and afterwards we had a class talk about dyslexia.

'Not yet, we're still applying for funding,' says Miss Monday. She's kneeling at the next table over, which is where she always goes right after we start writing because Jude sits there and Jude is the worst writer in the class.

I don't mean he can't spell or remember full stops or anything like that. And his handwriting is all loopy and old-fashioned. The trouble is, Jude never writes more than about one sentence. After that, he freezes like an old computer. It makes Miss Monday flap around him saying things like, 'It's more important to have a go than to get everything right,' and, 'If it's not hard, you're not learning.'

'Well done on writing three words on your own, Jude,' says Miss Monday. Three words? I've done nearly a page already.

I look over at Vanessa's book. We're neck and neck, only Vanessa's story is much better than

mine. Vanessa's really good at English. In her old
school she was in the top set and she gets ten out of
ten on every spelling test and last week her story
had three semicolons.

'So, you've introduced the main character,' Miss
Monday says to Jude. 'What is he doing?'

'He's mixing potions because that's how he does
magic, only he used the wrong ingredient and now
the potion looks like old tea,' says Jude. Jude is Black
with cropped hair and round glasses that make his
eyes look bigger than they are.

'That's brilliant,' says Miss Monday. 'Why don't
you write that down then?'

'Write what down?'

'That sentence you just told me,' Miss Monday
says. Her voice creeps higher whenever someone
asks a silly question. 'I'll be back in five minutes
to see.' And she walks away to check on Marcus's
spelling.

Cautiously, Jude loops another pristine word into
his book. Then he grabs a rubber from the pencil
pot and scrubs his page until it crumples.

'Jude, oh no!' Miss Monday hurries back. 'You'd
made such a good start.'

Jude puts his arms over his book and stares

14

down. His cheeks turn plum and his eyes go wet. Miss Monday touches his shoulder, but then Lila puts up her hand and Miss Monday hurries away.

I look up from Jude and catch Vanessa staring at him too. Then her eyes flick to me.

'Is that your story, Emmy?'

'Er…' Obviously it is, but I don't want her to read it. She'll think it's rubbish.

'Let me see,' she says and, before I can stop her, she grabs it and starts reading in a dramatic whisper. *'Once upon a time there was a waffle in a cardboard box…* you know this doesn't make sense, right?'

'Once upon a time there was a wizard in a castle,' I explain.

'That's not what it says, though. And you've forgotten to use commas. And 'because' isn't spelt like that.' She tuts. *'Then one day an evil drainpipe set the cardboard box on fire.'*

'Evil *dragon.*'

'You can't hand this in, Emmy,' she says. 'You'll get in so much trouble. Miss Monday will probably call your parents and say you need to move down to Year One.'

My face is burning.

'Unless I help you.' Vanessa taps her pen on her perfect freckled chin. 'I could correct it for you, if you like.'

'Vanessa, give it back. *Please.*' But I only half mean it, because what if she's right? I really can't spell 'because', and I don't know where commas are meant to go. Maybe I should be down in Year One with the tiny kids.

'Trust me, you're going to worship me for this.' Then she puts big pen lines through everything I've written so far and just starts writing. And I watch her. I don't know what else to do.

A shadow looms over the table. Miss Monday glares down at us.

'What exactly is happening here?' Her voice is ice-cold and I shiver. Vanessa smiles a sickly-sweet smile.

'I was just helping Emmy out, Miss Monday.'

'I didn't ask her to,' I say, desperately hoping Miss Monday believes me. 'She just took it and crossed out my story—'

'Well, it was a *bad story*, I'm trying to *help*,' Vanessa snaps.

'You know that's not how we do things at this school.' Miss Monday is being scarily calm. 'Now, give Emmy's book back, please, and come to my desk, I'd like a word with you.'

Vanessa throws my book at me and slams her chair back.

'Fine. It's not my fault you put me on the stupid table.'

'*Vanessa!*' Miss Monday's voice is sharp and loud and now the whole class is silent. 'We do *not* say things like that. It's unkind and untrue.'

Miss Monday looks as fierce as the obsidian dragon in the Sworshling Swamp. Her nostrils flare as if she's about to breathe fire. Vanessa snatches up her workbook and stomps to the teacher's desk and Miss Monday's eyes don't leave her the whole time.

After Miss Monday has had stern words, Vanessa collects her pencil case from our table and goes to sit in the empty seat opposite Lila.

Miss Monday claps her hands. 'Marcus, Emmy, Jude. Over here please. I've had a brilliant idea.'

Jude and Marcus look terrified. I don't blame them. When dragons have brilliant ideas, it's usually bad news for humans.

When we reach her desk, Miss Monday says, 'I've decided to try a little experiment. Instead of

handwriting this week's story in your books, why
don't you all go to the computer room and type up
your stories? Together! What do you think?'

I stare. Escape the torture of writing and
muck around on computers instead? Doesn't seem
possible. Marcus and Jude look as shocked as I am.

'I'll call Mr Gordon and tell him you're on your
way.'

THREE

To get from our classroom to the computer room, we go down a flight of stairs, across the hall, through the doors that link the old, draughty part of the school to the brand new, shiny bit, and up another flight of stairs. We couldn't be further from Miss Monday and the rest of the class. It's epic.

Marcus leads the way. He's the sort of boy who does all the talking in group work and wears a big watch that bleeps a lot. When we reach the deserted computer room, Marcus picks a computer and logs on before me and Jude can fetch our stools.

'Get your own,' he says.

'We're meant to work together,' I protest.

'Yeah, Miss Monday told us.'

Marcus huffs. 'Well, I'm doing the typing.'

AKAKAK went the guns over hed as Marcus
the hearo crowched on mountin redy to leep
up any moment now **THERE COMING DUK**
skreamd the sarjent as **SMASH** missile blue up
mud and guts flyeing evrywher

I look at Jude. His eyes have gone extra wide
behind his glasses.

'Marcus?' I say.

'Mmm?'

'I think some words are missing.'

'Mmm.'

He keeps typing.

'Marcus?' I try again.

'Mmm?'

'It doesn't make sense.'

He slams the mouse and spins round.

'Do your own story if you don't like it.'

When Miss Monday told us about Marcus's
dyslexia, I felt sorry for him. Now I feel annoyed.

Mr Gordon, who teaches Year Three, pokes
his head round the door. His face is bright red, but
then it's always bright red.

'Everything alright in here?'

'Yes, Mr Gordon,' says Marcus quickly.

'Miss Monday getting rid of troublemakers, is she? Well, keep the noise down, my lot are doing a test.' And he disappears.

'Marcus, if you don't let us help, I'm telling,' hisses Jude.

'Fine,' Marcus snaps, his voice low. 'Tell. I don't care. You're both losers with no friends and I don't need you.'

Jude's face crumples.

If only Marcus had shouted. Mr Gordon would be straight back to tell him off.

'We don't need you, then.' I slide off my stool and go the other side of the room, hoping Jude will follow.

Before I start writing my story, I can't resist having one tiny check on Islandr, just in case there are any new comments on my video.

'You play Illusory Isles too?' says Jude, hopping up beside me. 'That's awesome.'

'Of course I play. It's the best game ever,' I say, as the website loads. It always takes much longer on the school computers.

'I'm trying to bind the Mulch Queen before the new game comes out...' Jude starts, but I don't hear what he says next. On the Islandr front page

is a frozen image of Emmentine shooting fiery
sparks from her mouth. The headline says:

NEW FEATURED VIDEO: Top gamer binds Mulch
Queen without taking a single hit

That's me! That's my video!

Wobbles zigzag around inside me. Happy
wobbles criss-cross with worried wobbles. Before
I can speak, Jude says, 'I've got to see this,' and
presses play. Emmentine runs across the screen
and the Mulch Queen's fist slams down so hard the
speakers buzz.

'Too loud!' says Jude, hitting the mute button.

'That's my video,' I whisper.

'Huh?'

I cough. 'Um, that's my video. I made it.'

Jude twists to face me. 'You mean it's not real?'

My face goes hot. 'It *is* real. I bound the Mulch
Queen without getting hit once. That's my fire
elemental, Emmentine.'

I don't know if I should say all this. What if
Jude doesn't believe me? What if he tells everyone
I'm lying about making a video that got featured
on Islandr and the whole school makes fun of me?

But what if one real-life person—just one—knows the other me? The me who plays games and makes videos and fights Mulchbeasts and wins?

'Wait, I want to see the whole thing.' Jude starts the video again, watching in silence as Emmentine dodges the Mulch Queen's flailing arms, as she casts Cone of Repulsing Flame, as the crystals flash and the vines snap around the Mulch Queen. My hands shake and my knees jiggle.

'I can't do it,' Jude breathes, when the video finishes. 'I can't work out how to activate the crystals without getting smashed to pieces.'

'I've practised loads of times. And I spent ages levelling up too.'

'What level is Emmentine?'

'Level twenty. Don't even bother fighting the Mulch Queen unless you're at least level fifteen.'

'I've seen videos where people are only level eight but they've got lots of companions,' says Jude.

'I've never really done it with companions.' I clamp my hands on my knees. They're less jiggly now. 'I always save my most powerful attack for when the enemy is just too weak to fight back. That usually wipes them out.'

'I'm not very quick at fighting. I'm best at

making potions.'

'I tried playing as an enchanter once, but I kept forgetting the potion recipes.'

'I have a special notebook my dad got me. Every recipe I try, I write it down so I know for next time whether it makes a potion or not.'

'Wow, that's really organized.'

'Yeah, I wish I was better at fights, though.' He sighs. 'So that elemental is really, honestly you?'

'Really honestly.'

He gazes at the screen. Emmentine is frozen, mid-attack.

'So, will you add me on Islandr?'

'Er, sure?'

A grin explodes over Jude's face. 'That's so cool,' he says, a bit too loud. 'Islandr friends with Emmentine.'

Marcus whips his head round. 'Mr Gordon could come back, you know.' Marcus isn't even doing the work, he's playing a game which involves moving a fleet of submarines underwater to shoot at other submarines.

'Shall we write a story, then?' Jude whispers.

Jude tells me what to write, while I type it up as fast as I can. Sometimes he has to tell me how to spell different words, but I don't mind. I'm not like Marcus. And sometimes I have to block him from hitting the delete button because he thinks the story is rubbish.

'It's not rubbish,' I tell him. He doesn't believe me, but I pull the keyboard away so he can't erase it all in a panic like he does in normal English lessons.

'I wish we got to come to the computer room every English lesson,' I say, when it's nearly time to go.

'I wish we got to come here all the time,' Jude says. 'It's not as if anyone uses it at lunchtimes.'

'Yeah, that would be great. We could play Illusory Isles at school.'

'And you could show me how to fight the Mulch Queen!'

'We'd never be allowed though.'

Jude taps his chin thoughtfully but doesn't say anything.

FOUR

At school, we have a top playground and a bottom playground. The older kids mostly play on the top playground, which has goalposts and a shelter with benches and monkey bars where there's always a queue.

I sit on the wall by myself and daydream about Illusory Isles II. I've watched the trailer hundreds of times already. There are going to be giant churning maggots and ruined temples full of Mulchbears. There's a town full of colourful flags but no people, and a cave where flapping beasts swoop down out of nowhere. It's going to be amazing.

In my head, I'm Emmentine. Mulchbeasts swarm the sky and scurry at my feet, but I swipe and roar, burning them up with my fiery spells. I leap onto the wall and summon a Cone of Repulsing Flame, 'Rawr!' Mulch creatures reel back, their singed bodies sinking into the ground below.

'Off the wall, young lady. It's not safe,' says the teacher on duty. 'Where are your friends?'

I shrug and jump down with a thud. I don't have an answer, but the teacher doesn't wait for one. She's already telling off a boy for using a skipping rope as a lasso.

Vanessa, Ria, and Lila are standing on a bench nearby practising their dance routine for the summer fayre. They're doing the same moves as always, with the zigzaggy arms and stompy feet. I watch for a moment, but I'm no good at dancing so it's probably better that I don't play with them today.

'Hey, Emmy, can you do this?' shouts Vanessa. She does this dance move where she kicks her right leg and spins in a circle. It's impossible to do without falling over, but Vanessa and Lila can both do it as easy as walking. Even Ria doesn't fall off the bench when she tries.

'Not really.' I pick at the cuff of my fleece. Last time I tried, I fell over and got grazes on both knees. It was Vanessa's first week, and she'd just joined dance club with Lila, and she said we should all practise their routine. I kicked and span, fell right off the bench, and had to go to first aid for two plasters.

Vanessa smiles. 'Try it, though.'

'Nah.'

'Why not?'

I scuff the tarmac and shrug. Vanessa knows why not. She saw.

'You not doing anything else, are you?' Behind her, Lila and Ria shuffle one way, then shuffle back.

'Suppose not,' I say. Vanessa isn't the sort of person you can tell about destroying the mulch with cones of repulsing flame. Whenever me and Lila wanted to play pretending games last term, Vanessa said we should dance instead, until we stopped playing pretending games completely.

'Don't worry, Lila will show you how. Won't you, Lila?'

I copy the way Lila stands, feet apart, hands on hips. I'm not going to fall over this time.

Lila kicks and spins. I kick and get halfway round and my legs are tangled up, but I do an extra kick and put my hands on my hips as if they were there the whole time.

'I did it! I actually did it!'

Vanessa raises one eyebrow. 'Only sort of. You nearly fell over. Again.'

'No, I didn't.' My face is hot.

Ria flumps down onto the bench. 'It's probably your shoes.' Ria is big and glittery all over. Her dad buys her this expensive make-up which she brings into school for Vanessa and Lila to borrow.

'My shoes?' I look down at my shoes. They're the same ones I've always had, Ryan's old shoes with the Velcro straps and peeling-off rubber. 'What's wrong with them?'

'They're just a bit ... well, rubbish.' Vanessa snorts.

'Yeah, maybe if you get trainers like ours you wouldn't fall over,' says Ria. Vanessa's trainers are black and Lila's are purple and Ria's are shiny gold, but they're all the same style, with big rubber soles and logos and bright laces tucked behind the flap.

'Um.' We could never afford brand new trainers like that. 'But I like my shoes,' I say. Which was true until about five seconds ago.

Vanessa looks down. 'Aren't they boys' shoes? I've never seen any girls wear shoes like that before. Not in my old school, anyway.' This is the sort of thing Vanessa always says. She used to live in a city, where everyone was way cooler than here.

'They're my brother's,' I explain.

'You'd look better if you got shoes like ours. She would, wouldn't she, Lila?' asks Vanessa.

'Yeah, much better,' Lila agrees in that quiet voice she uses now she's Vanessa's best friend.

'I know I would,' I say. I wish I could, too. Then I could be a proper part of their group again.

'So, why don't you?' Vanessa asks.

In Illusory Isles, if you want to change how your character looks, you just go to the nearest inn and talk to the innkeeper, and then the character wardrobe page pops up. But in real life it's not that easy.

I shrug. 'Don't know if Mum'll buy them.'

'Why wouldn't she?' Vanessa asks, like I've said something weird. Maybe I should have said something else. 'Ria's dad buys her make-up whenever she wants.'

Ria nods. 'He does, actually. It's because he loves me so much, he'll do anything to make me happy.'

'Oh, right,' I say. I don't think Mum can afford to buy me anything I want.

Vanessa gives me a pitying look. 'Do you get all your clothes from charity shops or something? I bet that fleece is from a charity shop.'

'It isn't.'

'Then why is it so old?'

I nearly tell her. I nearly say that most of my clothes used to belong to my brother or cousins. But I bet no one from Vanessa's old school wore passed-down clothes. So I don't say anything.

'Well? Can't you even answer an easy question?'

My skin is burning. Even not answering is the wrong answer!

'What if the last person who owned your fleece peed on it?' asks Ria.

'Gross.' Lila giggles. I can't believe she's going along with this.

'No one peed on it. The fleece is from my brother too.'

Vanessa smirks. 'Well, it actually stinks of pee.'

I try to take a step back, but Vanessa follows. 'Why would my brother pee on his own fleece?' I say. She's right up close so I have to take another step back.

'I was only joking.' Vanessa laughs, right in my face.

'Yeah, can't you even take a joke?' says Ria. The whistle goes for the end of break, but they don't head inside. It's like Ria and Lila are waiting for permission.

31

'Just, if I wanted people to like me, I wouldn't wear a fleece like that,' says Vanessa. She strides off with Ria and Lila hurrying behind.

IslandrChat

IndigoChalice

Have you seen the new trailer? The Mulch Queen is coming back!

MeowMeow

NO I THOUGHT SHE WAS DEAD

Emmentine

I new shed be back. shes way too powerful

MeowMeow

But she was buried in a cave by her own magic. I thought she'd suffocated or been eaten by Mulchworms???

Emmentine

go and watch the trailer!!! she bursts right out of the ground. I AM SO EXCITED

FIVE

Even though I know Ryan never peed on my fleece, when I put it on at home time I can sort of smell whiffs of wee. I really hope it's coming from the boys' toilets, not from me.

Our house is only two corners and one zebra crossing away from school, so I'm allowed to walk home by myself. Dandelions sprout in the cracks between the pavement, so I pick some to give to Pie, our rabbit.

In the back garden, I stroke Pie's black ears as the dandelion leaves wiggle into his mouth. His hutch smells a bit of wee, but that's because he's a rabbit.

As soon as I get inside, I pull off Ryan's old shoes and Ryan's old fleece and heap them on the kitchen table. I grab a school letter tacked to the wall about a theatre trip last term. On the back I write:

Don't want these any more

I put the note on top of the shoes. Handwriting is my worst thing, but I write really carefully, so Mum can definitely read it.

I grab the biscuit tin, then go to check my Islandr comments. I have to refresh the page in case there's a mistake.

1,078 comments, 3 direct messages.

I haven't received that many messages ever, in my life, all added up. Over a thousand! Is this because my video got featured? What if people hate it? I've seen people get trolled before when their video went viral. My fingers tingle as I open the messages.

crimsonwarrior
Woah, you didn't take any damage!

Ezalita4dreams
YOU ARE ILLUSORY INCREDIBLE

Me55yh3ad
ur some kind of genius ive shown this to evry1 i no

I did it! Everyone loves my video! I stuff a biscuit in my face and hardly even chew. I bet Vanessa has never done anything like this. I bet no one at school has. A thousand comments. About something I did.

Wow.

Inbox

Islandr Team
Congratulations on your front-page feature!

me55yh3ad
can u sho me how to make a video

IslandrTeam
Opportunity to help on new Islandr project

The first direct message is just letting me know my video has been featured, as if I could miss it. The next message is someone asking me to help them make a video. Me! Because people think I'm an expert video-maker now.

I send me55yh3ad a list of tutorials I used to learn, then open the final message.

Dear Emmentine,

The Islandr team loved your video, **Binding the Mulch Queen – NO DAMAGE!!!**

We are planning a video tour by Islandr members to celebrate the release of Illusory Isles II, and we'd love you to contribute. The videos will be featured on the website, so it's a great opportunity to get noticed!

If you want to get involved, let us know and we'll feature your video on the tour.

Cavedancer
Islandr Community Volunteer

My eyes slide over it so fast I can't take the words in properly. I eat three biscuits at once to calm myself down.

Then the back door slams open. Ryan's home! I rush to the kitchen, to find him chucking his blazer and bag on the floor.

'Ryan, come and read this message for me. I'm not sure what it means.' I drag him towards the computer.

'Emmy,' he complains, but he comes anyway.

'There.' I do a jiggly dance around the room as Ryan reads. My mouth is full of the dry, sweet aftertaste of biscuits.

'You numpty,' he says eventually, and I stop mid-jiggle. 'They're just saying you're really good at playing that Illusory Isles game and they want you to make another video.'

'Yes!' I punch the air, 'yes, yes, yes,' and jump, jump, jump around the coffee table.

Ryan shakes his head, but he's smiling, so I know he's at least a bit happy for me. 'Yeah, yeah. Good for you. Are you done with the computer? I've got history homework.'

'Let me reply first.' I scrabble for the seat before he can get it.

Dear Cavedancer

I would LOVE LOVE LOVE to make a video about Illusory Isles II for Islandr. I'm really excited for monday when we get to finally play it!!!

Emmentine

By the time Mum and Paul get home, I'm in the garden playing my own version of Illusory Isles with Pie. I am Emmentine, fearsome fire elemental with big teeth and dagger-like claws, and Pie is a deadly Mulchrabbit terrorizing the enchanted forest where valuable ancient scrolls are buried (he does this by hopping around in the hedge and digging a burrow).

'Emmy? Come here please,' Mum calls.

Mum and Paul are in the kitchen. Paul's eating a pork pie from the fridge. He's the only one who likes pork pies, so he buys them just for himself.

'What do you mean you don't want these any more?' Mum holds up the shoes and fleece.

'I just don't. Can I have new ones?'

'You know we can't afford it.' Mum throws herself on one of the kitchen chairs, all slumpy. 'And two people didn't show up for their appointments today, so that was practically the whole day wasted.' If people don't show up to get their tattoos done, Mum doesn't get any money. 'They're still good shoes, Emmy, no holes or anything.'

'They're too small,' I say.

'Rubbish. Show me your feet.' I sit next to

Mum and stick my foot up. Mum lines the shoe up against my sole. 'Loads of room, see?' It was worth a try, I think, as mulch starts to guzzle up my braincells.

'But they're boy shoes.'

'Well, so what?'

'People say things about them.'

'Mean things?' Paul asks.

'They say I'd look better if I had shoes more like everyone else.'

Mum stands up. 'We don't have the money, Emmy. Maybe after the summer holidays.'

'That's months!' I say. The time stretches out before me like a long sludgy road I have to wade along. Wearing horrible shoes.

'Just hold on until September.' Mum picks up the shoes and the fleece in a pile and hands the whole lot to me. Then she yanks open the snack cupboard and sighs. 'Paul, is there any chocolate?'

'You two could stop eating pork pies and chocolate for a few weeks,' I tell her. 'We'll be rich in no time.'

Paul shrugs at me and shoves another pork pie in his mouth.

SIX

That night I throw the fleece and shoes into Ryan's room, but in the morning I find them in a pile in the hallway.

The next day, Ria turns up wearing a jacket just like Vanessa's, but bright gold to match her trainers.

After school, I stuff my fleece and shoes in the bin, but Mum finds them out and hands them to me with a look that says she's just not having it. After going in the bin, the fleece really does stink.

On Thursday Lila comes in wearing a new jacket in silvery-grey. I don't even wear my fleece. I decide I'd rather be cold than stinky. By the time I get home, my fingers are a weird grey colour.

'Veggie lasagne tonight,' says Paul. He's at the sink, scrubbing the chopping board.

'Yes!' Homemade lasagne is my favourite. 'No peppers?' I ask, remembering to fetch cutlery from the drawer.

Paul's face falls. 'Oh no!' he says. 'It's all peppers.'

I stare at him in horror, a fistful of cutlery in each hand.

He cracks a grin. 'Got you,' he laughs. 'You should see your face, Emmy, I know you hate peppers.' I'm glad I can't see my face. My cheeks feel hot and my mouth is hanging open.

Our kitchen isn't big, but it's very cosy. The counters are always cluttered with mugs and piles of bills. The best bit is the wall behind the table. It's covered with Blu-tacked paintings by me and Mum and Ryan. Before Paul moved in, we would sit round the kitchen table on rainy Sundays doing art projects. Then we stuck our creations on the wall. Our last project was designing our own monsters. There's my lionicorn, and Mum's sunflower flamingo at the top, and Ryan's cannon-dragon is further down, shooting cannonballs from its mouth.

We haven't done a rainy Sunday project since Paul moved in, but just seeing all the pictures on the wall makes me feel safe, like there's a storm outside, but I'm not in it.

That's not the only thing that's changed. Unlike Mum, Paul knows how to cook.

The lasagne comes out sizzling with a crackly top and gooey cheese underneath, and the smell soon brings Mum and Ryan to the kitchen. As we sit down, Paul lifts out a perfect lasagne cube.

'How do you do that so neatly?' I ask.

'Magic,' he says. He places the cube on my plate. 'Chances are I'll mess the next piece up,' says Paul. And he's right, the next one slides about and ends up a sloppy pile in front of Ryan. 'Sorry, kiddo.'

'It's fine,' Ryan says, but he pokes at it like it's slug jelly.

Mum plonks peas on both our plates. 'How was school? Was anyone nasty about your fleece and shoes today?'

'They weren't trying to be nasty,' I say. 'They were just trying to help. Why can't I have trainers like everyone else?'

'We can't afford them.' Ryan drags out the sentence like a nagging grown-up. 'It won't make a difference, anyway. People are mean because they want to be mean, not because there's anything wrong with your shoes.' Ryan is cutting his lasagne up into chunks without even eating it.

'Don't be negative, Ryan.' Mum drops some pasta on her jumper, scoops it off with her finger and sticks it in her mouth anyway. 'Perhaps Emmy doesn't want to wear her big brother's hand-me-downs for the rest of her life.'

'But a few days ago you said—' Ryan starts.

'Well, I've had a think since then, haven't I? Emmy, we've got a surprise for you,' says Mum.

Eagerly, Paul gets up from his seat. 'I'll get it.' He disappears into the hallway, but returns moments later, clutching a plastic bag. On the side, it says SPORTSMALL in big red letters. SPORTSMALL is the sort of shop that sells golf balls and tennis rackets, so we never shop there.

'I popped into town on my lunch break,' says Paul, 'and I saw these on sale.' He sticks his hand inside the bag and pulls out a gleaming pair of new trainers. A yellow sticker says 50% OFF!

I can't believe it. I never get anything new.

I reach for the trainers. They're white with chunky orange soles and orange laces. They've got a big logo stitched on the side. Vanessa's going to be knocked dead when she sees them.

'There's more,' says Mum. Paul rustles in the bag again and pulls out a jacket. It's shiny and black, almost exactly like Vanessa's.

'Saw it in the window of Oxfam,' says Paul. I hold out my arms and he passes it over. 'Careful you don't trail it in your cheese. Is it the right kind of thing?'

I push one arm through a sleeve, waggling my fingers out the other end. Already my hand looks as if it belongs to someone older and cooler.

'It's fantastic,' I say. 'And the trainers too. It's all fantastic.'

Mum and Paul are both grinning. Only Ryan glares at the shoes as if they've told him he has a big nose.

'What do you say?' says Mum. I'm holding up the jacket, watching it gleam under the light.

'Thank you! Thank you so much, Paul.'

'Do you want to try them on?' Paul says. 'We could have a fashion show.'

'This is stupid.' Ryan drops his fork with a clatter.

'Ryan?' says Mum.

'New shoes aren't going to change anything, Emmy. People aren't going to be friends with you just because you're wearing trainers.'

He's wrong. I know he's wrong, because

Vanessa said so.

'Ryan,' Mum snaps. 'Emmy asked for the trainers. Paul is trying to do something helpful.'

Ryan stands so abruptly his chair falls back and hits the wall. 'I told you, it won't help.' The cannon-dragon picture comes unstuck and drifts down to the lino. 'You know it won't help, Mum. But no one listens to me, not now Paul's around.'

'Ryan?' Mum calls, as Ryan stomps away down the hall.

'Paul isn't our dad, you know. We don't need a new dad.'

'Ryan, wait—' says Mum.

But Ryan slams his bedroom door.

Paul gives a big sigh. 'How long has that been brewing?'

Mum puts a hand on his knee. 'Emmy, do you want to try these on, so we can see?'

I start to pull on the jacket.

'In your bedroom, Emmy,' says Mum, giving me a tight smile.

Oh, they want to have one of those private adult chats. I clutch the jacket and shoes to my chest. As I run upstairs, Mum says, 'Ryan's just being a teenager. He'll get used to it,' but I think there's more to it than that.

Most of my bedroom carpet is taken up with a cardboard model of the Illusory Isles that Mum and Ryan helped me make. There's the star-shaped Isle of Shimmer, the smallest, with its enchanted forests and silver wolves. There's Sheen, the biggest island, with its bustling city and big lake. And then the last island, Shade, the one we don't know much about.

I leap over the models to sit on the bed. I pull the trainers on, carefully tying the orange laces behind the flaps like Vanessa does. I zip the jacket up to my neck.

Awesome.

Mum and Paul wait side by side in the hallway. Mum gasps as I appear on the landing. Paul smiles so wide that his ears stick out.

'Looking good,' he says.

Hands in pockets, I swagger down. Or at least I try to. It's hard to swagger on a staircase.

I catch my reflection in the glass of a photo hanging on the hallway wall. It's a school photo from years ago, when Ryan was my age and I was still in the Infants. Both versions of me are layered on the glass. Little me in the photo, with my fussy uniform and goofy grin. And on top, the reflection of me now. Cool, older me, my fringe grown out, my hands in my pockets, wearing clothes that for once never belonged to Ryan.

'How do you feel?' says Mum.

I feel happy and braver and bigger and like I could take on anyone. My hands feel tingly like I have magic powers now and Mum looks so happy and Paul looks so hopeful that I fling my arms around him in a huge hug.

He feels round and solid, and he smells spicy from cooking. Up close, I notice speckles of tomato sauce on his T-shirt.

And I want to let him know that I've noticed how much he does to help Mum out, and how he makes Mum happy, and I know how much effort he makes to cook us food we like and everything.

But I don't know how to say all of that without sounding weird, so I just say, 'Thank you for the clothes. They're amazing.'

'I hope they help,' says Paul, letting go.

'Come 'ere.' Mum drags me into another hug. Her hair tickles my neck.

And I want to burst into Ryan's room and tell him he's wrong about Paul, that making lasagne with no peppers and buying trainers is totally different from how Dad was when he lived with us.

But I don't, because this is a happy moment. So instead I ask, 'Is there ice cream for pudding?'

IslandrChat

IndigoChalice
Pals—Islandr are looking for new volunteer moderators, do you think I should apply?

MeowMeow
YES GO FOR IT

Emmentine
that wuld be so good, you can do your own feature videos and weekly highlights and stuff like CaveDancer does

---

IndigoChalice
CaveDancer is a community volunteer. That's the next step up. I'll just be stopping fights on the messageboards.

MeowMeow
Youll be a community volunteer in NO TIME, you're so good at that stuff.

LEVEL UP:
INITIATE

SEVEN

On Friday morning I put on my gleaming new trainers and shiny new jacket. It's raining, so Mum offers to walk me to school.

'I'll bring my rainbow umbrella.' She puts it up, and we march out into one of those warm, wet mornings where the air smells of damp leaves.

As we turn onto Poplar Lane, we join a crowd all heading to school in their colourful raincoats and wellies.

'Isn't that Lila?' asks Mum. 'Do you want to run ahead?'

It is Lila. Her curly hair hangs down the back of her silvery jacket and she's sharing her frog umbrella with a girl in the year below, chatting away. It's been ages since I've seen Lila so chatty.

'You're friends with Lila aren't you?' says Mum when I don't answer.

Am I? Before Vanessa came along, me and Lila's

favourite game was called Superheroes. We each had a superpower, like being able to fly or breathe underwater or having mega brains, and had to use our powers to save the school from evil.

'Sort of,' I say. Hopefully, by the end of the day, we'll be proper friends again.

'Lila!' Ria runs past us and snatches Lila's frog umbrella to hold it over her own head. 'You'll never guess what—' but the rest is lost in the crowd's babble.

I tuck my hands in my pockets and flick back my hair. At break time I'll show them my jacket and trainers and they'll see I'm just like them.

■ ■ ■ ■

In Maths, I keep my feet tucked under the table. I want my new trainers to be a secret until break time.

All I can think about is the look on Vanessa's face when I walk towards her in my new jacket and shoes. In my imagination I'm wearing sunglasses, even though I don't own sunglasses. Vanessa's mouth will hang open and she'll say, 'Nice shoes, where did you get them?' and it won't be a trick question, and Lila will say, 'Do you want to play

the Superheroes game?' and Ria won't know what
to say.

But by break time the rain is even heavier and
Miss Monday tells us it's too wet to play outside.
I can't believe it! It's the first time I've looked
forward to break time in forever and we're stuck
in the classroom.

Marcus gets out the chess board and starts
telling everyone else how to play. Jude fetches a
wordsearch from his tray and doodles on the back
of it. Ria asks Vanessa to play four-in-a-row, but
Vanessa says, 'No, I want to finish this book.'

'What book is it?' asks Lila.

'It's the new book by Jemima Crown,' says
Vanessa, '*Supersonic Girl.* You remember I told
you all about her other books? Well, this one's
about a girl who can travel faster than sound.
That's mega fast.' As Lila peers at the book cover,
Vanessa grabs the sleeve of her cardigan. 'Lila,
why are you wearing this again?'

'It's cold,' says Lila, looking as if she wants to
yank her arm away.

'I thought we weren't wearing cardigans any
more.' Vanessa drops Lila's arm and starts to
read.

'We weren't?'

'No,' says Ria, 'because I bet they don't wear cardigans in Vanessa's old school. Do they, Vanessa?'

'That's right,' says Vanessa, turning the page.

■ ■ ■ ■

'You know what you said before? About wishing we could go to the computer room all the time?' Jude says, as we head through the empty school, during English.

'Yeah?'

'I had an idea. What if I ask Miss Monday to do a lunchtime club? Computer Club. Or we could call it something better than that.'

'Keyboard Wizards. IT Ninjas. Geek Gang.'

'Exactly!'

'That would be cool,' I say, bouncing up the stairs to the Year Three corridor.

'Shhh!' Marcus is marching ahead, not speaking to either of us. We walk in silence for a moment.

'Do you think we could play Illusory Isles?' I say, after a moment.

'That would be epic,' says Jude. 'Did you see that teaser video for Illusory Isles II? The one with the swamp creatures?'

'Yeah, and there's a hole right through its belly and it just regrows itself in seconds,' I say. 'How are you meant to fight that?'

In the computer room, the air con drones like a swarm of flesh-eating bees.

'Marcus, you can work with us if you want,' I offer, but he shakes his head and stomps to a computer by himself.

Our story is just getting to the exciting bit now. It's about an elemental and an enchanter from Illusory Isles who discover that the Mulch Queen has been making secret spells that turn people into Mulchzombies.

'And the zombie leader has a third arm that once belonged to someone else and he's carrying three axes,' says Jude.

'And wherever the zombies go they leave a trail of stinky slime that turns the ground to mulch,' I say.

The heroes are running from the zombies through Sheen City, but they've just hit a dead end.

'The sinister procession glided closer,' says Jude in his storytelling voice. *'Emmentine dodged, but JadeMage was too slow. As the enchanter slid on the*

sopping slime, Emmentine grasped his robes and pulled him free. His dragonhide boot hissed and melted away with a smell like sulphur.'

It turns out Jude is a very good storyteller.

As we walk back to the classroom with our printed story, I can't stop reading it over and over. Jude knows lots of interesting words like *contorted* and *sepulchral* and he knows how to spell them too. When he tells a story, he sounds exactly like a book.

'I don't like the ending,' he complains.

'Why not? It's the best ending Miss Monday will have ever seen in the history of the world.'

'I've thought of a better one.'

Marcus has already vanished when we reach our classroom.

'Hello, you two,' says Miss Monday, sitting at her desk. She holds out her hand for our work, reads a bit and smiles. 'Nice! What lovely description. *Sepulchral*, I like that word.' I puff up. 'This looks very exciting. It reminds me of some of my favourite books.'

'Most of the writing was Jude,' I admit.

'But Emmy came up with the exciting bits.'

'Well done, both of you. You should be really

proud.'

'And we had an idea.' It bursts out of Jude like Mulchbats from the Caverns of Carn. 'What if there was a club for going on the computers? At lunchtime, I mean. We could play games or make videos…'

Miss Monday adjusts her glasses. 'That's a good idea. I'll have to talk to Mrs Trimble, see what we can come up with. Aren't you bright sparks today?'

In the cloakroom, I say, 'She's going to do it!'

'A real computer club at our school!' Jude pumps his fists.

And the rain has cleared, and I pull on my gleaming new jacket to show Vanessa I'm cool now, like her. Today is turning into a really good day.

EIGHT

The sun sneaks through the grey clouds and makes the damp playground glitter. It's like the end of Illusory Isles, where everything is shiny and colourful.

I cross the tarmac, winding through the rush and bash and scream of everyone else. I am untouchable. My black puffy jacket gives me Super Strength. If anyone gets in my way, bam, they're blasted to outer space. My shoes have Megaspeed. I could run twice around the school, *flash*, in a nanosecond. It's like when I used to play Superheroes with Lila last year.

I start to run. I skid through puddles, punching and kicking and elbowing, and then I *dash, dash, dash* at hyperspeed, until I fly into the air and over the playground, and then *smack*, I run into someone's back.

'Oof.'

'Sorry,' I mutter, rubbing my chin where I bumped it. The person I bashed into wears a gold jacket and has thick black hair in French plaits. Ria.

'Watch it,' Ria puts a hand on her hip and scrunches up her nose. It's like she's been practising looking superior in a mirror.

But I'm not worried, not now I have my own jacket and my own new trainers. I put my hands in my pockets and straighten up, hoping she'll notice.

Ria looks me up and down. I grin.

'Oh Em Gee, Vanessa, look, I told you.'

On the wall, Vanessa is showing Lila something in a notebook. Vanessa snaps her notebook shut. I wonder what sort of secrets she writes in it. Is it all about how she hates this school and she's cleverer than everyone? Is it about boys? Maybe she uses code...

'Emmy, what are you actually wearing?' Vanessa asks.

'New trainers. Like you told me. And I got a new jacket too ...'

'That's not new.' Vanessa jumps down and grabs my sleeve. 'Look, it's got a stain.' My guts twist in a knot. We all stare. It's only a tiny mark, but beside hers, my jacket looks scruffy. My superpowers dribble away. 'Did you get it from a charity shop?'

'Um.' The answer is yes. But yes is the wrong answer. So I don't say it.

I think about telling her I'm internet famous. That my video has been watched by over a thousand people. That I'm way better at Illusory Isles than she'll ever be. But I don't want her to know about that, because it's exactly the sort of thing she'll say wasn't cool at her old school.

'Yuck,' says Vanessa. She drops my sleeve like it's a dirty tissue. 'This jacket smells worse than your pee fleece.'

'Eeuurgh,' says Ria, loving it. Lila squeals and covers her mouth with her hands.

Vanessa puts her head on one side. 'Are your mum and dad too poor to afford anything new?'

I shake my head. 'It was a present from my mum's boyfriend.'

'Oh, yeah, Lila said,' says Vanessa in a voice like she's talking to someone ill. 'Your dad lives in Scotland, and he doesn't even send you Christmas presents. That must be why you're a bit weird.'

'North Wales, actually,' I mutter. My nose is full of weirdness and I don't know how to say he sends gift vouchers instead, and I can't believe Lila told Vanessa. Only a minute ago I could have blasted Vanessa away with my Super Strength and run away with my shoes flashing deadly fireballs from the soles, but now it's all ruined.

Vanessa leans in close. 'At least Ria's dad takes her to India every summer. He's always buying her new stuff too.' Ria flashes her earrings. 'Do you ever visit your dad in Scotland, Emmy?'

I picture our visit to Dad in North Wales last summer. It was raining the day we went to the beach, but we went bodyboarding anyway. Ryan says Dad's better now he doesn't live with us. Dad doesn't mind doing fun things and he doesn't yell.

Then I picture Paul with his huge grin, clutching a dish of homemade lasagne.

But I don't say anything, because whatever I say it always comes out wrong.

'Vanessa!' Ria says, pointing at something. My shoes. 'Oh, this is good!'

'Lila, look!' says Vanessa. 'She's got the same trainers as you.'

My chest feels tight. Surely that's a good thing? Lila is Vanessa's friend now. But when I look at Lila's trainers, they're the same purple ones she was wearing last week.

Lila's face flushes.

'Like those ones your mum bought you that we realized were totally ugly, remember?' says Vanessa.

'Orange laces and everything,' says Ria.

Vanessa asks, 'Have you still got them, Lila?'

'Yes,' mouths Lila. She shakes her curly hair over her face. I can't help but look at my trainers sitting next to Lila's purple ones, and Vanessa's sleek white ones, and Ria's gold, sparkly ones. The orange is beaming out a message, *loser, loser*. It's even worse than wearing second-hand boys' shoes with Velcro fastenings.

My jacket cuffs cling to my wrists, the trainers bite my toes. I want to tear them all off and throw them over a wall and run and run.

My eyes prickle.

'You could wear yours tomorrow, Lila,' Vanessa says. 'Then you and Emmy would be ugly twins.'

I swipe at the corner of my eye where there's a blob of water. I wish Lila and me could be a team again and save the school with our Megaspeed trainers.

Lila is crimson. Her grey eyes dart between

Vanessa and me.

Then her face hardens.

'Gross! As if I would want to be anything like Emmy.' She tosses her curls back and puts her hand on her hip, just like Vanessa. 'I'm going straight home to burn those ugly trainers. They've got Emmy disease.'

Another water blob runs from my eye and I smack it away.

'Emmy disease,' repeats Ria with a grin. 'Good one.'

I look at Lila for help, but she just smirks.

'Is it some kind of brain disease?' says Vanessa. 'Is that why you have to do English on a computer? So it can do the writing for you, because you can't do it yourself?'

'I *can*—'

'Like how I used to help you all the time, before Miss Monday moved me onto a table with cleverer people?'

I want her to stop talking and I don't want to be here and I want Lila to help and I want to reload to a time before Vanessa came and made everyone think I was stupid by telling them about how I'm not good at writing and I want to run away with Lila and play games like we used to.

I think of all the games me and Lila used to play. Scouting for enemy soldiers in the big play equipment. Stopping Mrs Trimble, the headteacher, from conducting alien experiments on the Infants. That time that we discovered a dragon cave, and at first we tried to slay the beast, but then we realized she was only angry because she couldn't play games or bake cakes with her giant dragon claws, so I helped with the controls while Lila baked strawberry cupcakes.

I tie all these memories in a thought-ball and throw it through the air from my brain into Lila's. I almost see the ball disappear through her hair into her earhole.

Lila's smirk falters, and I'm sure it's worked. Then the whistle goes for the end of break.

Lila stares at me for a moment longer than the others. Her smirk says it doesn't matter what I do. I'll never be their friend.

NINE

The spitting rain grows heavier, and by home time it's tipping. I sprint home with my arms over my head.

Each step I take, I hear Lila's voice in my head saying my trainers have Emmy disease. The mulch is right behind me, swallowing the street, and even though my bright orange trainers shoot fireballs to stop it, the mulch is too powerful.

When I reach home, I race upstairs, tearing off my soaking jacket. I kick off the trainers, bundle them up and stuff the lot under my bed, as far back as I can.

I shake my wet hair. Droplets fly across the room and dot the cardboard model of Sheen Isle. I pull on my comfiest pyjamas, my biggest jumper, and my fluffiest socks.

Downstairs, I grab the biscuit tin before sitting at the computer.

Lila's face floats in my brain, right at the moment she said Emmy disease.

I squash her face flat. Go away, Lila, you're not allowed in my head any more.

On Islandr I have a new DM.

 Exclusive Offer for Islandr users - 20% off Illusory Isles II when you buy in the first week! Just use this promotional code at checkout . . .

This is perfect! Mum will be able to buy Illusory Isles II and she might not even have to give up eating chocolate to save money.

I copy the code onto a blank document, but it looks a bit bare. So I add some pictures of elementals, enchanters, and Mulchbeasts from the internet and print it out.

I give it to Mum later that evening. She's in the kitchen with her sketchbook open, drawing a dragon. It's ice blue with spiral horns and icicle teeth. I wish I could draw like Mum.

I put the printed code beside her sketchbook. 'What's this?'

'It's a promotional code for Illusory Isles II.'

'Oh,' says Mum.

'You know, the new Illusory Isles game? It's out on Monday, and it's a lot cheaper if you use the code. Twenty percent cheaper.'

'That's not bad,' says Mum.

'Yeah, it's brilliant. Probably enough left over for five chocolate bars, at least. And you know my video? The one I made of Emmentine beating the Mulch Queen? Well it got featured on Islandr and loads of people have watched it and I've been asked to make a video about the new game for a special video tour.'

'That's great, Emmy,' says Mum.

'So I'll really need the new game as soon as it comes out,' I say. Mum hasn't promised to buy it yet. She's concentrating on shading the dragon's scales from dark blue to light blue.

I wait, but she's too busy drawing. She says when she's doing art time disappears for her the same way it disappears for me when I'm playing video games.

'Nice dragon,' I say.

'I've got ideas for all sorts of new dragon tattoo designs,' says Mum. She draws smoke curling from the dragon's mouth.

'There are dragons on the Illusory Isles,' I

tell her. 'On the Isle of Sheen, mostly. They're elemental, so some are made of flowers and leaves, and some are made of crystals.'

'That would be interesting to draw,' says Mum.

'Could you really do an Illusory Isles tattoo?'

'I can do anything,' Mum says.

'My lionicorn?' I say, pointing to the picture on the art wall.

'Anything.'

I watch as she adds a puff of smoke curling from the dragon's mouth.

'Well, I should probably practise my spellings,' I say, tiptoe-bouncing towards the hall.

'Emmy?' I look back. Mum's waving the code in the air. 'Don't you want this?'

'No, Mum, it's for you. To buy the game with when it comes out on Monday.'

Mum frowns at the piece of paper. 'Oh, right. I didn't realize. Thanks.'

I jump all the way upstairs. She's going to buy it! I can't wait!

■ ■ ■ ■

On Sunday I wake up from dreams of Emmentine fighting a giant frog that looks like a cross between a Mulchbeast and Lila's umbrella. The sky is blue and my chest fizzes with excitement.

Only one day until Illusory Isles II comes out.

And then I'll make a video. Something impressive. Maybe I'll be the first to discover a monster hidden behind a secret doorway or I'll win a fight with a combo that shouldn't be humanly possible.

I roll out of bed and clatter downstairs. Mum is watching TV in her pyjamas. Ryan sprawls on cushions on the floor.

'Tomorrow! It's coming out tomorrow!' I run into the room and jump on the sofa next to Mum.

'Ow,' she says as I land on her foot. 'What is?'

'That game she's always on about,' says Ryan. 'Improbable Isles, or whatever it is.'

'Illusory Isles II.' I kick his head with my bare foot. 'It comes out tomorrow and I can't wait.'

Mum growls like a bear. 'Too early. Too loud.'

'I wish I could just go to sleep now and wake up tomorrow, so I could play it straight away,' I say. 'Even though I'd miss half the weekend, I don't care. I want to play it now.'

Ryan laughs exactly one laugh. 'Who do you think is going to buy it for you?'

'Mum is.' I frown. Ryan's just trying to spoil it for me, because of big brother rules. 'She already said, when I gave her the promotional code yesterday. Didn't you, Mum?'

'What?' Mum blinks like she's just woken up from hibernation.

'You're going to buy Illusory Isles II tomorrow. Aren't you?'

'Oh, Emmy.' Mum rubs her face with one hand. 'For your birthday perhaps. But we don't have the money for new games right now.'

TEN

My throat closes up. I breathe in hard, out hard.

'But, Mum.' My voice is almost a whisper.
'I need Illusory Isles II tomorrow. You don't
understand. I have to make a video.'

'Emmy, you can't have everything you want the
moment you want it.'

I breathe in, out, harder. I *know* that. I *don't* ask
for everything the moment I want it. Other kids
get mobile phones for their birthdays, but I've
never asked for that. They go to clubs like dance or
violin that cost money, but I've never asked for that
either.

Illusory Isles II is different.

'Mum, I won't be able to go on the internet.'

'Don't be ridiculous.'

'No, I mean all the things I normally do, all my
online friends. They'll all be talking about it. And
I won't have played it, so I won't have anything to

say. And I've been asked to make a video, but I—'

'Emmy.' Mum cuts me off. 'Your birthday is next month. We can't afford it until then. End of discussion.'

Ryan raises his eyebrows at me as if to say, *told you.*

I scramble off the sofa and run to find Paul.

He's in the garden, pegging damp underwear to the line.

I take a deep breath and stretch out the skin of my face with my hands. I don't want to look cross, or Paul will know I've just argued with Mum and he'll take her side without even listening.

'Paul, you know Illusory Isles II is out tomorrow?'

'You've mentioned it.' He pegs up Ryan's Star Wars boxers.

'And, what with the video I've been asked to make and everything—' I'm tangling my hands around themselves and twisting my legs together and I try to make myself stand normally, but I can't remember what normal standing feels like. 'I need the game as soon as it comes out. It's super urgent.'

Paul has pegs in his mouth. 'Ha'e you aske'

your mum?'

'She doesn't realize how important it is. Paul, could you ask her?'

Paul disappears behind a cartoon sheep tea towel.

'It's up to her really, Emmy.' His face appears again, pained. 'You've just got some new clothes too. You might have to wait, kiddo.'

I rush inside.

Stomp, I go upstairs and *smash*, my bedroom door flies back and *thud, thud, thud* go my feet as I pace across the floor. I pick up my Mulch Queen doll and *smack*, it hits the wall and chips the paint, and then I grab the model of Sheen Isle, and *crunch*, it crumples and crashes down onto my bookcase. I snatch my cuddly Emmentine lion and I'm about to throw her as well—

But I can't.

I squeeze her in my arms, and I squeeze my eyes shut, and I throw myself on the bed and try to squeeze myself into the mattress.

After a while, my cheeks don't feel as hot. I can breathe again. I want to cling onto the anger and keep raging, but it drains away. I shiver. My face is wet.

74

I can see the chipped paint on the opposite wall from here. Mum'll kill me if she sees. I dig out my poster paints at the bottom of the cupboard.

I squirt out blue and red onto an old spellings sheet and mix them together to try and make purple, but it goes a bit brown. I slop paint on the white spot and try to blend the paint into the wall behind. It sort of works. If I step back and squint, the wall looks just the same as before.

There's a knock on my bedroom door.

'We're off to the shop, Emmy,' says Mum's voice. 'Do you want to come, or stay here with Ryan?'

'Stay,' I croak.

'You could pick something nice for your lunchbox.' I don't say anything in case it's obvious I'm still bunged up with tears. 'Are you OK?' Mum pushes at the door slightly, and I say, 'I'm fine,' quickly so she won't come in and see the mess.

The door stops moving.

'Back in a bit then.'

I don't want it to be tomorrow any more. I want it to be Sunday forever so no one ever gets to play Illusory Isles II and I can just talk to my online friends forever and so I never ever have to go back to school.

Thinking of school reminds me of the orange trainers, and how they have Emmy disease.

Maybe I can fix them.

I dig the bundled trainers out from under my bed. They smell damp and mulchy. I squeeze out a big blob of black paint.

The paint doesn't stick to the trainer very well unless I make it really thick. I splodge black all over the orange soles. I pull out the orange lace, painting one side black then rolling it over to paint the other. My fingers are covered in paint. I lean over to pull out the second trainer from under the bed.

When I sit up, I see it: a big black handprint on the carpet.

Mum's going to murder me.

I run downstairs.

'Ryan!'

Ryan is in the living room, headphones on, watching something explode on the screen.

'Ryan, help.' I nudge him with my elbow. As Ryan turns around, I hold out my paint-black hands towards him.

He sighs. 'Emmy, what have you done?'

'Come and look.'

When I open the bedroom door and stand back, he gazes around, unimpressed but not surprised.

'What happened?'

'I was painting,' I reply.

'Painting what?'

Ryan's eyes flick round then rest on the trainer, now oozing a black footprint onto the carpet next to the shape of my hand.

'They were too orange,' I mumble. 'Vanessa said they were ugly.'

Ryan sighs again, but it sounds kinder this time. 'I knew Paul's present wouldn't work.' He goes to the airing cupboard and pulls out the oldest, tattiest towel, stained purple from Mum's hair dye. 'Who exactly is Vanessa?'

'She started at Christmas. I think maybe she doesn't like me or something.'

'Well, then she's a loser,' he says, walking to the bathroom.

'It's 'cause I'm bad at English. She was annoyed because Miss Monday sat her on a table with me, and she's good at English and I'm not.'

'Being better at English doesn't make her a better person. She's a numpty if she thinks that.' He runs the towel's corner under the hot tap and squirts apple shampoo on the damp bit. 'You should stand up to her, you know.'

'Like how?'

'Like, say stuff back. Show you're not scared.' Ryan goes back to my room, lifts the paint-covered shoe and places it carefully on a spare bit of scrap paper, then scrubs at the stained carpet with the towel.

'What, say that Vanessa's jacket smells of ... smells of poo?'

'Yeah! Anything. I used to have trouble with this kid last year. Then I told him he smelt like a goat and rapped like my Granddad, and he left me alone.'

'Didn't you also punch him?'

'That too.' Ryan shrugs. 'He doesn't bother me any more though.'

'So, I should punch Vanessa?'

'If it makes her stop.'

Ryan scrubs and scrubs at the carpet with the towel and eventually the black disappears.

'Ryan?'

'Mmm?'

'Why don't you like Paul?'

Ryan sighs and scrubs some more. Then he says, 'You were only two when Dad left. You don't remember what it was like when he lived here. We're better off with just the three of us.'

'But Paul isn't like Dad. He makes Mum happy.'

'Bet he won't forever, though,' says Ryan gloomily. He bundles up the towel and pushes it to the bottom of the laundry basket. I expect him to go back to his explosions, but he stands gazing at the glistening patch of painted wall.

'Mum'll spot that a mile off, Emmy,' he says, but the way he says it is like a non-player character on Illusory Isles explaining the next quest, not like he's telling me off. He wipes the wall with toilet paper and the poster paint washes straight off. 'I think the old tester pot is in the cupboard under the sink.'

After Ryan digs out the tester pot, I replace everything in the cupboard in the same order we took it out, just in case Mum notices things have moved. Then I go to the front room. I open my Islandr inbox. I don't want to do this.

Dear Cavedancer,

I really really wanted to make a video but I can't. we can't afford to buy illusory isles 2 so I won't be able to play it or make a video.

I'm really sorry.

Emmentine

I click send. For a moment I think about going back and putting a handprint on the floor on purpose, to show Mum what she's done.

But then she won't even buy Illusory Isles II for my birthday.

Ryan comes back downstairs.

'Don't suddenly decide to paint your whole bedroom again, will you?'

'I won't. I promise,' I tell Ryan's feet. 'You won't tell Mum, will you?'

'Of course not. I promise.' He gives me a big-brotherly arm punch and goes back to his explosions.

When I get upstairs, I find that Ryan has cleared everything up. My toys are lined up neatly on the bookshelf. When I kneel down I see the painted trainer on some newspaper, hidden behind my box of Lego. On the wall is a tiny wet purple spot, so small you'd barely notice.

ELEVEN

On Monday morning, the day Illusory Isles II is released, I put on Ryan's old school shoes. I try not to think about the trainers hidden under my bed, one splodged with black paint.

I sniff my new black jacket. I can't decide if it smells weird or not, so I sneak into Mum's bedroom. I find a bottle of perfume and spray a few puffs onto the jacket.

The pong stings my nose. My jacket definitely smells weird now. I stuff it into the laundry basket.

'Where's your new jacket?' Mum asks, as I shrug on my fleece by the front door.

'In the wash. Mum, please can you buy me Illusory Isles II?'

'Yes—for your birthday. Come on, Ryan left ten minutes ago.' Mum puts her coat on and grabs her bag.

'But he gets the bus. And the promotional code

only works this week.'

'Here are your sandwiches.' She hands me my lunchbox and opens the front door. I only have seconds to convince her.

'Mum, it's really important.'

She nudges me onto the front step. 'Look, Paul only bought you that new jacket and those new trainers last week, and you're not even wearing them.'

'But—'

'No, Emmy.' And she shuts the front door behind us.

So that's that. Never mind that my online friends will totally abandon me. Never mind that I've let Cavedancer down. Never mind that I had the chance to be really famous on Islandr, but now I never will.

I go to school already feeling like my tummy is sloshing with mulch and I might puke up grey slime any moment.

Hopefully over Vanessa's shoes.

At break, I lie down on a bench. My belly swims and I'm getting that cold tingling in my skin that always makes Mum say I look pale. Maybe I'll ask Miss Monday to send me home.

'Emmy?'

I jump, but it's only Jude.

'Are you alright?'

'I think I'm ill.'

'Oh.' He sits on the bench. I move my feet to make room. 'Illusory Isles II comes out today, did you know?'

'Obviously. But my mum won't buy it.'

'Why not?'

'Says I can have it for my birthday next month.'

'But that's way too late!'

'I know!' The swishiness stops swishing for a moment and I sit up. 'And what's even worse is that Cavedancer from Islandr messaged me and asked if I would make a video about it, and I said yes, but now I can't.'

'That's completely rubbish,' says Jude.

We both sigh and watch some Year Threes play skipping.

It's nice that someone gets it.

'My parents bought me Illusory Isles II this morning,' Jude says. Way to rub it in. 'I actually started downloading it so it'll be ready as soon as I'm home.' My stomach wriggles again. Jude looks at me like he's waiting for something.

84

'Thing is,' Jude says, snapping and unsnapping the bottom popper of his jacket, 'I just wondered, well, if you were feeling better... I just wondered if you wanted to come over to mine tonight? We could play Illusory Isles II together?'

My chest fills up. It's too full to breathe.

'I'll have to ask my mum,' I say at last.

'OK.'

'She'll be at work.'

'OK.'

'But I know her mobile number off by heart.'

'OK.' Jude unsnaps his bottom popper and snaps it closed again, snap, snap. He's being very awkward, even for Jude. 'Um, so, did you want to come over then?'

'I definitely a hundred percent do. Please, I mean.'

Jude grins and my bad stomach disappears in an instant.

■ ■ ■ ■

At the end of school, I rush Jude out to the cloakroom, shove my lunchbox in my bag and grab my coat from the peg. I want to get to Jude's house as fast as possible. I want to play Illusory

Isles II right now.

'Come on, come on, come on,' I bounce around Jude as he slowly puts the homework in his bookbag.

'Hang on, I have to find my PE kit.'

'Argh.' I fling coats and shoes and PE bags around, but I don't know what Jude's PE bag looks like and I know I'm just making a mess.

At last, we hurry across the playground to the crowd of waiting parents.

'Who's this?' says a voice. I stop and stare at a glamorous lady wearing tight pink trousers and enormous, jangly earrings. It can't be Jude's mum—can it?

'This is my friend, Emmy,' says Jude. She is Jude's mum! Her hair is streaked with purple. My mum's hair is purple too, but my mum isn't glamorous, she's just weird.

'Of course! Nice to meet you, Emmy, I'm Sonja. I'm so happy Jude has made a new friend.'

'Please can she come over, Mum?' Jude asks.

'Please, please, please,' I beg. Usually I'm shy with grown-ups I don't know, but Illusory Isles II has taken over my brain like a fever, and also Jude has told his mum that we're friends, and I can't stop bouncing.

After Sonja has called my mum to check it's alright, she leads us to a spotless silver car.

'Do you like make-up, Emmy?' she asks after we climb inside. 'I sell make-up. I've got some lovely eye-shadow palettes that would go beautifully with your cool skin tone. Or fake nails?' She waves her own turquoise nails on the steering wheel. 'Do you want nails like mine?'

'Um—' My knees jiggle. Vanessa would say yes. Vanessa would know the exact sort of nails that would look cool. Part of me wants to say yes—to swagger into school tomorrow, flashing my fake nails at Vanessa, Ria, and Lila. But another part of me knows I would choose the wrong colour and they would just make fun of me.

I look at Jude for help and he rolls his eyes.

'They would get in the way of her gaming, Mum. Emmy is a superstar gamer. She'd break her nails on the gamepad.'

'Oh, that Illusion Island game,' Sonja sighs. 'Jude only ever thinks about Illusion Island. That or his plastic models.'

'It's *Illusory* Isles,' says Jude.

'People get addicted to computer games you

know,' she warns.

'Yeah, but not games like Illusory Isles. Anyway, it's good for strategic thinking.'

'Yes, so your dad keeps saying.'

'What's strategic thinking?' I ask.

'Like, working things out logically and planning ahead.'

'Oh yeah, you have to do that all the time in Illusory Isles,' I tell Sonja.

We drive all the way past the big supermarket to the new estates with their curving roads and tidy lawns. Jude's front door is bright white with a shiny brass number 30. It seems very posh. Our front door has peeling green paint, and if you want to know what number it is you have to look at the giant 8 painted on the wheelie bin.

Inside, Jude's house is spotless. Jude takes off his shoes and nudges me until I do the same. Through the living room doorway, there's a cream sofa with bright cushions, each in exactly the right place. A huge flat screen TV fills one corner. There are no old cups of tea and no abandoned socks.

Jude turns to me, his eyes bright. 'Illusory Isles II?'

'Woohoo!'

We sprint upstairs, whirl round the banister and burst through a door into a gloomy room. Jude leaps across the cluttered carpet and switches on another flat screen TV, which sits on top of a chest of drawers. It's not mega big like the one downstairs, but it's still bigger than our TV at home.

There are socks on Jude's bedroom floor. And T-shirts, jeans, a pair of pants, and lots of tiny bits of plastic. It smells of paint and I wonder if it's just been decorated.

The TV screen lights up, already showing the Illusory Isles II store page.

'Yes! It's finished downloading.' Jude drags two beanbags against the opposite wall, grabs a game controller from a pile of mess on the carpet. 'I'm so excited.' I bounce over clutter, and I've nearly made it to the beanbags when something stabs into my foot.

'Ow!' I say as Jude flings open one of the curtains. I pull out the thing from my foot and squint at it.

It's a tiny plastic man with a long grey beard and crimson robes covered with tiny symbols. His staff is bent from where I stepped on him.

'Sorry.'

'Don't worry, it's just a warlock. I've got loads more.' In the streaming afternoon light, I see that the floor is strewn with miniature figures.

'What are they?' I pick up another model which looks like a knight riding an armoured bear.

'Warsorcery models.' Jude shoves the nearest ones on top of the drawings on his desk. 'It's this tabletop game. You create an army of little plastic people and then fight someone else's army. I don't really have anyone to play against, I just like to paint them.'

'You painted this?' Even the creases of the warlock's face have been shaded in, and the whites of his eyes. 'It's amazing.' More tiny, colourful models are clustered on his bookshelf and bedside table. 'How do you do all the details?'

'Practice.' Jude shrugs and flops down into one of the beanbags. 'Do you want to have the gamepad first?'

'Oh.' I'd forgotten you could play Illusory Isles on things others than a computer. I've never played with a gamepad before, only a keyboard, and I'm sure I'll press the wrong buttons and end up bashing Jude's character into a wall or a tree. 'No, you go first.' I drop onto the beanbag beside him. 'After all, it's your game.'

'Do you want to make a new character?' asks Jude, as the game menu pops up.

'No, I want to see yours. You're an enchanter, aren't you?' My knees won't stop jiggling, making the beanbag crunch.

'Yeah, I just really like finding all the potion ingredients and trying different combinations.'

Jude's enchanter spins on the screen. His beard is plaited in a long blue braid, and he wears a thick leather belt, with all sorts of bottles hanging off it. 'Aren't bottle spells really annoying to throw?'

'They have a big range and they can damage whole groups of enemies. Once I froze a whole swarm of Mulchspiders in ice,' he tells me smugly.

'Well elementals don't need to carry bottles to do spells. They can do amazing combos, like dazzling the Mulch Queen to immobilize her then doing a big fire attack.' I retort. 'Plus, fire elementals light up in the dark.'

Jude sticks out his tongue at me. I grin back. I'm buzzing. I never get to talk about Illusory Isles like this, in real life, to someone who knows as much as I do.

Jude taps a button. The theme music starts, frilly flutes and churning strings, and all my attention is on the game.

This is it. Illusory Isles II. Months of suspense end now.

TWELVE

The normal Illusory Isles theme tune mixes with new sparkling and crashing sounds. The screen fades up from black as it launches into a cut-scene.

It's the cavern of crystals on the Isle of Shimmer. The Mulch Queen struggles against the vines that bind her. The swampy floor bubbles around her, sucking her down until she vanishes. The scene jumps to a place outdoors, with cracked flagstones and bleached trees. Suddenly the ground erupts, and vines, thorns, and dirt spew out.

Jude gasps. 'It's the Mulch Queen!'

The four-armed monster hurtles from the hole. Her pondweed hair leaks slime. Her rotten teeth curl over green lips. She stamps and the ground shakes. She roars and the sky fills with whirling insects.

The Mulch Queen stands in a vast castle carved into a mountainside. Huge pillars and arches are strangled by clinging thorns or sink into pools of slime.

'The Mulch Queen's fortress,' says Jude. 'It's huge!'

My knees jiggle. I clutch one knee in each hand, but they won't stay still.

Tiny insect specks zoom across the land. Wherever they go, woods and meadows rot away, buildings crumble, and vicious monsters roam about.

The mulch is spreading.

Finally, the view sweeps down onto the neighbouring island, Sheen, and in through the window of a pointed tower in the city. Inside, the room glows, full of polished wood and velvet curtains. A group of five elders stand in a circle: an elemental, an enchanter, a fighter, a healer, and one of the fair folk.

They look very serious.

'She's taken the Isle of Shade,' the healer rumbles. 'She must be stopped.'

'But who can stop her?' asks the fighter. 'We've all tried.'

The door flies open, the five elders turn. Through the archway strides a figure with blue hair and bottles hanging from his belt.

It's JadeMage.

The screen goes black. We stare at each other.

'We're going to see the Isle of Shade at last!' I wriggle on my beanbag.

'There are supposed to be some really rare ingredients on Shade.' Jude's eyes are wide. 'Things we've never seen before.'

'So JadeMage will get to make completely new potions? That's so cool. Aren't the ingredients expensive?'

'Not if you know where to collect them yourself,' he says, but he's interrupted by sea swishing and birds cawing and jaunty fiddle music. The game has begun.

JadeMage leaps off a ship onto the docks on the Isle of Shade. It's night, but the port is alive with coloured lights and music. Ahead, there are market stalls and dancers and jugglers.

Clutching the gamepad, Jude pushes the thumbstick forward and JadeMage strides along the docks. As he passes sailors in their striped trousers, speech bubbles pop up over their heads.

That must be the hero sent from Sheen.

As if one person can defeat the
Mulch Queen.

I just hope she leaves well alone while
the Mystic Market's in town.

'The Mystic Market!' we say at the same time,
and I know my mouth is as wide as Jude's.

JadeMage runs past fishing boats and sailing
ships into the market. He weaves round jugglers,
fortune tellers, and tantalizing stalls. Bottles clink
on his belt and his dagger waggles on his thigh.

Then a shriek rips through the air. Black wings
block the sky and talons hurtle between market
stalls. A Mulchbird!

'Run!' I say. JadeMage swerves around the
creature and stumbles into a pastry stand. Cakes
roll across the cobbles. The beast screeches again.
'Now attack.'

'Trying,' says Jude. JadeMage grabs a bottle.
The Mulchbeast swoops down, and we catch a
glimpse of its poisonous green eyes.

'Throw it now!' I yell. 'Now!' as the bird
creature shoots past. Jude fumbles with the button,
and the beast is already gone by the time JadeMage

flings his bottle. It bursts on the road, burning with blue fire. The townsfolk flee.

'Sorry,' says Jude, turning JadeMage round. My fingers twitch. Suddenly I'm itching to have a go. JadeMage swipes with his dagger and hits. The Mulchbird falls back.

'Another potion.'

JadeMage stabs again. 'Sorry!' says Jude. He taps another button and JadeMage flings a bottle. This time it hits, smashing on the Mulchbird's steely beak. With a cry, the beast dissolves into green smoke.

I punch both arms in the air. 'You did it! Yes!' Light swirls around JadeMage as he levels up.

Jude wipes his forehead with his sleeve. 'Take that, mulch.'

'Amazing!'

'Now to find an apothecary.'

As Jude trades gold coins for herbs and powders, I hear the sound of tyres crunching on the drive. I jump up to look out the window, in case it's my mum already.

The car on the drive is long and shiny. A round man in a suit, who must be Jude's dad, slams the car door and walks towards the house. On the street behind him, a group of kids on scooters sail off the kerb and loop around each other on the dead-end road. I watch them trace a pattern on the tarmac.

On the row opposite, a door opens and a girl steps out. Long gingery hair swishes past the shoulders of a lime green tracksuit.

It's Vanessa.

She pulls a scooter from the hallway and swoops around the street with the other kids. A teenage girl with the same reddish-blonde hair shouts something from the doorway, but Vanessa ignores her, soaring towards Jude's side of the street.

I duck under the windowsill, nose to the wall.

'Look at all these ingredients,' says Jude. 'Starflower. You can make a Time-Stop Tincture with that. And redfrond and torberry. I wonder what those do.'

I turn, but I can't focus on the screen.

'Jude, what's Vanessa doing out on your street?'

Jude is engrossed. 'What?'

'Vanessa. From school. She's standing on your street right now.'

'Yeah, she lives at number twenty-three. We helped them move in by making them cups of tea

98

when they couldn't find their kettle. Her mum works with my dad.'

'What?' Suddenly Jude's safe, cluttered bedroom seems grey and swampish. There's a knot in my throat.

'You're friends aren't you?' he asks. 'I've seen you together at break.'

'No. No! Definitely not friends.' I press my back against the cold wall, and I know I'm staring at the screen, but I don't know what I'm looking at.

'Oh. Well.' says Jude. 'I sort of am.'

My mouth hangs open. It just does it by itself.

'You're friends? With Vanessa?' I blink. 'I've never seen you together.'

'More like outside-school friends. My mum hangs out with Vanessa's mum, so then I hang out with Vanessa. She's quite good at Underfleet, but she doesn't like Illusory Isles.'

'Oh.' I slide as far down into the carpet as I can.

'Sometimes she wants to pretend to be Supersonic Girl and she makes me play the other characters, only I haven't read most of Jemima Crown's books so I always get it wrong.'

I try to imagine Vanessa pretending to be a superhero, but I can only picture her bossing Jude around. 'Well. She's always mean to me.'

'Oh,' says Jude. I wait for him to say something else. Something like, *only joking, I hate her, or I'll stop being her friend right away*. But he doesn't. Instead, he carefully counts how much knotvine and blueroot he needs, then starts crafting potions.

'OK, JadeMage's ready now,' he says at last. 'Where should we explore?'

JadeMage strolls out of town, past the fairy houses up the hill and the derelict shacks where the mulch has invaded the town. He circles a swamp dotted with grotesque statues and, by dawn, he's sailing over a lake of Mulchfish that leap from the water with bulging eyes and curved teeth.

Soon JadeMage reaches a thick forest of tall, needly trees. The game music changes to low jangling notes.

'You do the next bit,' Jude says. 'The music is going all creepy and dark, so something bad is about to happen.'

'You've done creepy bits before,' I say to be nice, but actually I really want to play, even if I get the controls wrong and run into a tree.

Jude hands me the gamepad. I grip it in both hands, trying to copy the way he wrapped his fingers round the sides. I press each button with my right thumb, to test what they do. JadeMage jumps, draws his knife, and crouches.

It's not so hard.

JadeMage runs downhill through the trees until he bursts into a circle of standing stones.

The stones are carved with swirly symbols and sunlight bounces off a mosaic of red and gold on the floor. I'm so busy looking at how pretty it is, I don't notice the looming shape nearby.

'Mulchbear!' shouts Jude.

But I'm fast. JadeMage grabs a glittering blue bottle and whoosh, it flies into the Mulchbear's belly and bursts into piercing ice crystals. JadeMage is already reaching for another bottle as he dashes at the creature. The bear raises its paws to strike. Green slime drools from its mouth. JadeMage raises the bottle, ready to smash it down—

And I press the wrong button. JadeMage crouches. The Mulchbear's claws swipe over his head, just as I hit the right button and *crash*, the bottle bursts and flames pour out from the bear's nose and ears. He burns up from the inside, until nothing is left but ash.

'That was *epic*.'

'I know,' I say, like I did it all on purpose. 'I didn't realize Enchanter's spells were so powerful.'

'Only if you hit. If you miss, you've wasted them,' says Jude. 'Hey, what's that noise?'

The noise coming from the game sounds like someone gasping for air. JadeMage spins round and sees a person tied to a standing stone, struggling against the ropes. The ropes cut into her emerald robes and her mouth is gagged. But before we can go over, there's a shout from downstairs.

'Emmy!' Sonja calls. 'Your mum's here.'

I can't help groaning.

'Will you come again?' asks Jude. I hesitate a moment as I remember Vanessa standing on the street, and Jude telling me they were friends. 'We can find out who that tied-up person is together. I won't play any more without you,' he promises.

'Obviously, I'll come,' I say holding out the gamepad.

IslandrChat

Emmentine
Guess what? I was just playing illusory isles 2

MeowMeow
HOW????!!!! I thought your mum wouldn't buy it?

Emmentine
Round a friend's house. We killed a mulchbear.

MeowMeow
OMG tell me how. I'm COMPLETELY stuck on the bear.

Emmentine
We were playing as an enchanter not an elemental so we used potions. Youll work it out.

MeowMeow
Ha. Ha. You know I won't.

THIRTEEN

Mrs Trimble, the head teacher, always wears weird outfits. In today's assembly, she's wearing an orange dress with a green cardigan and green shoes. She's even wearing green and orange earrings. She looks a bit like an alien trying to blend in with humans.

'I have a grand announcement,' she says, once everyone's quiet.

'Maybe she's going to announce that we're being abducted to her home planet for alien brain experiments,' I whisper to Jude. Now that I have someone to sit next to, I get why other people can't resist whispering. Even when they're not meant to.

Mrs Trimble bobs up and down like an excited pumpkin. 'Springhill School is having its very own writing competition!' Typical. I sigh and pull up the Velcro on my shoes.

Mrs Trimble babbles on about rules and

deadlines and where to put the entries. The last thing she says is, 'We're very lucky to have a special person who will decide the winning entries—none other than famous author, Jemima Crown!'

Gasps from behind me. Vanessa squeezes Ria and Lila's arms. 'Ohmygod, ohmygod, ohmygod,' she whispers. 'I am so going to win.'

Of course. She loves those Jemima Crown books.

'Everyone knows you're the best at English,' says Ria.

'You should definitely enter,' says Lila.

'I'm going to, obviously.' Vanessa smiles. 'You two can enter if you want, but I don't see why you'd bother.'

Her fingers squeeze their arms so tight she might snap their bones. When she lets go, Ria rubs her arm but Lila's trying not to show it hurts.

Jude fiddles with his laces. I nudge him. 'You should enter,' I hiss. 'Your story was as good as a real book, Miss Monday said so.'

'*Our* story,' he mouths.

'But most of it was you. I think you could win.'

'I'll think about it.'

Yes! If Jude enters, maybe Vanessa won't win.

■ ■ ■ ■

I want to talk to Jude about what story he could
write at lunch, but after circling the whole
playground twice I can't find him.

For once, there's no queue at the monkey bars,
so I leap up. I'm Emmentine, swinging through
the trees on the Isle of Shade. The standing stones
are up ahead, and there's the Mulchbear! With a
well-timed attack, Emmentine can knock him down
before he knows what's happening. Emmentine's
claws burn as she gathers a ball of flame...

Pow! The bear tumbles to the stone. Take that,
Mulchbeast!

'Who are you talking to?' asks Vanessa below
me.

I jerk my hand back. Vanessa, Lila, and Ria have
me surrounded. They look like evil superheroes
in their coordinated jackets and Vanessa is eating
a bag of cheesy crisps that she's meant to have
finished in the lunch hall.

'I wasn't talking to anyone,' I mutter. Was I
talking out loud? Did I look weird? I turn around
on the monkey bars to swing away, but Vanessa,

Ria, and Lila move round to block me.

'Watch out!' says Ria, as my knee swings. 'You practically hit me in the face.'

'I didn't, you moved in the way.'

'Emmy, get down before you hurt someone,' says Vanessa, and she licks orange cheese dust from her fingers.

'Yeah, get down.'

'Get down, Emmy.'

My arms and shoulders and belly ache from holding onto the bars, but I don't want to get down just because they tell me to.

I turn around again. They block me again.

'I don't like this attitude, Emmy,' says Vanessa, as if she's a grown-up telling me off. She crinkles up the crisp packet and drops it on the floor. 'We're just trying to be friendly. And you obviously need friends if you're talking to yourself.'

The skin on my hands burns. I let go of the bar and drop onto the rubber matting.

'So, *were* you talking to your imaginary friend just then?' asks Vanessa.

I think about running, but they're on every side so I can't get away.

'What's your imaginary friend's name?'

Ryan said I should say something back to them, show it's not a big deal. I squeeze my brain, hoping something clever comes out.

Vanessa leans next to me, her face up against to mine.

'I know. I think your imaginary friend is called Jude,' she says, too close, and a cloud of cheesy-crisp breath puffs over my face. 'Am I right?'

'Gross!' I don't even recognize my own voice. 'Your breath stinks. Brush your teeth, or someone will pass out from the smell.'

Vanessa jerks back.

'What did you say to me?'

'You should see a doctor or something, that's disgusting.' My heart thuds and my arms shake but I'm doing it, just like Ryan said to. I'm fighting back.

Vanessa straightens up. 'Did you hear what she said to me?' she asks Lila. Lila's eyes go wide. 'My breath doesn't stink does it?'

Vanessa breathes on Lila. Lila wrinkles her nose but she says, 'No, Vanessa.'

'Does my breath stink, Ria?' Vanessa asks, breathing on Ria's left cheek.

'Minty fresh,' says Ria, opening her eyes wide at

me.

Liars.

'What's Miss Monday going to say when she hears you called me stinky breath?' asks Vanessa, arms folded.

My heart jumps about.

'I didn't—'

'First you hog the monkey bars, then you tell Vanessa she stinks,' says Ria. 'That's not very nice, is it?'

I'm cold all over. 'But—'

'You're not exactly going to make friends like that, Emmy,' says Vanessa. 'No wonder no one likes you.'

'Jude likes me,' I whisper.

'No, he doesn't.' Vanessa rolls her eyes. 'Where is he, if he's such a good friend?'

I hug my arms round myself. I need to make her stop.

'You're a weirdo, Emmy,' Vanessa sneers. 'A weirdo who talks to herself.'

I've tried to make her stop again and again but this time I'll do it properly, just like Ryan said. I have to punch her. I clench my fist and it shakes and shakes.

'And Jude wouldn't be friends with a weirdo, would he?'

Before I can change my mind, I swing my fist at her face and *slam*, Vanessa's head jerks to one side.

She holds her hand to her cheek and the skin underneath is bright red. My heart beats so hard it might burst apart. I can't believe I punched her. Why did I punch her? It's going to make her so much worse.

'MISS!' Vanessa yells. Instantly a lunchtime supervisor is there as if Vanessa has the power to summon them, like the Mulch Queen summons beasts. The supervisor wrings her apron and says, 'Do you think your ought to go to First Aid? Who's your teacher? Can you go together?' I know I need to get my story in first, so I run past Vanessa and head straight for the cloakroom door.

Just as I reach the door, it swings out, nearly hitting my face.

'Emmy!' Jude stands there beaming. 'Miss Monday was just asking if I could make a poster for Geek Gang—'

But I push past him into the cloakroom.

The cool and quiet makes the angry redness beating in my head louder and bigger. I can barely see. I stumble through the classroom door towards Miss Monday.

Everything comes into focus. Miss Monday is eating tomato soup from a plastic cup. She's dripped some on the books she's marking.

'Miss Monday?' My hand is still tingling and somehow I feel angry and brave and also more scared than normal. 'Vanessa said mean things to me and I didn't know how to make her stop, so I—'

'Miss Monday,' Ria calls in a singsong voice from the doorway. She has her arm around Vanessa's shoulders and Lila holds Vanessa's free hand. Vanessa is clutching an icepack to her jaw and limping.

Limping? Seriously?

'She punched me,' Vanessa announces.

'Yeah, Emmy actually punched her. Right in the face,' says Ria. 'She might have broken Vanessa's nose. You should call an ambulance.'

Miss Monday takes off her glasses and rubs the lenses. Without them on, she looks tired.

She perches them back on her nose and looks at me so sharply that it's like tired Miss Monday was a figment of my imagination.

'Emmy, wait outside, please.'

FOURTEEN

Miss Monday talks to Vanessa for ages. I sit under the coatrack, looking at the messy floor. Then I decide, if I tidy up the cloakroom, Miss Monday might be less cross with me. So I hang up bags and coats and I put the shoes in pairs under the bench.

It's much neater by the time the door opens but Miss Monday doesn't come out. It's just Vanessa, fake-sniffling into her icepack, with Ria and Lila on either side.

'Miss Monday says to go in,' says Ria. I look around at the tidy cloakroom. Miss Monday didn't even come out to see it! I breathe in, but the air won't go in very far.

There are three chairs by Miss Monday's desk. Miss Monday points and I sit.

'I've written down Vanessa's account,' she says. 'Now I want to hear yours.'

The air still won't go in. 'I was on the monkey

bars, and Vanessa told me to get down even though
I didn't want to, then they wouldn't let me leave
and I tripped over and they said I was a weirdo
with imaginary friends.'

I wait for Miss Monday to write something
down but her pen just hovers.

'So did they actually do anything to you?'

Sometimes grown-ups aren't very smart at all.

'They surrounded me so I couldn't leave. They
said I was weird. It was the *way* they said it.'

'But Vanessa didn't actually hurt you?'

'Well . . . and also, my brother said if I just
stand up for myself, Vanessa might stop. She
always does this.' I don't think Miss Monday gets
what I'm saying.

'So she didn't hurt you, but you hit her?'

'I . . .'

The answer is *no*, she didn't touch me.

The answer is *yes*, she hurt my feelings. *Yes*, she
makes playtimes horrible every single day. *Yes*, she
tells me I'm weird but I don't understand why she
picks on me. I'm not the only person who's bad at
English. I'm not the only person who can't dance
or doesn't have cool clothes. I don't understand
why those things matter.

113

I wish Vanessa *had* hit me. Then she would be
in trouble, not me.

'Did she hurt you, Emmy?'

'I don't know,' I say. And it's true, really. I don't
know what Miss Monday wants me to say.

She sighs. 'You don't know.'

I look at the carpet.

She checks the clock. 'You can stay inside and
sharpen pencils as a consequence for punching
Vanessa. And I'll have to phone your mum.'

Mum is going to absolutely murder me.

What seems like hours later, Miss Monday tells
me to put the pencil sharpener away. I find my seat
for Geography. When the class comes in, all they
can talk about it how Vanessa got punched in the
face.

'I heard it was Ella-May from the other class.
You know how she used to punch people when she
was in the Infants?'

'No, it was obviously Ria. Remember Ria hit
that boy last year?'

'Only 'cause he called me fat,' Ria hisses.
'Anyway, it was Emmy. She just went off on one
for some reason.'

'I reckon Vanessa just got hit in the face with a

football,' Marcus mutters.

I don't talk to anyone for the rest of the day, even though Miss Monday makes us do projects in groups. I'm in the middle of making a temple from toilet rolls when Jude ambles up to my chair.

'Did you really punch Vanessa?'

'I don't want to talk about it.'

'You still coming over tonight?'

'Mmhm.' I hope it's true.

After school, in the cloakroom, Jude doesn't seem to notice I'm not feeling bouncy like him.

'And sometimes I make this special snack where you cut off a cube of cheese and you wrap it in ham and eat it just like that, I call them cheesy ham cubes, and I thought we could make them when we get back to my house.' He leads the way outside.

I gaze across the tarmac. There's Jude's mum in a bright orange dress. And standing next to her is my mum. Mum is wearing her work T-shirt, dungarees, and an expression that says, *you're in big trouble, young lady.*

'You're in big trouble, young lady,' says Mum, as soon as we get close.

'Why aren't you at work?'

'You know why. I'm going to take you home,

we'll have a talk, and then I have to go back to work. I'm going to have to work late too. And that's your fault, missy.'

'You *did* punch Vanessa, then?' asks Jude. I nod. He gets a worried expression on his face like I've just transformed into a Mulchbeast.

Sonja puts a hand on Jude's shoulder and pulls him away. 'Come on, Jude. Let's leave Emmy and her mum to their conversation.'

Mum doesn't speak until we're in the kitchen at home.

'Sit.'

I sit and stare at the table top. There's an old paint stain from when we used to do art projects. I scrape it with my fingernail.

Mum doesn't sit down. She paces from the sink to the table and back again.

'I had a phone call from Miss Monday today.' Scrape, scrape. My nail is clogged with blue dust. 'What do you think she said?'

I think about answering, but I can't. I scrape the last bit of paint off the table then I don't know what to do with my fingers.

'What do you think Miss Monday said, Emmy?' I shrug. Mum sighs.

'She told me you hit a girl, Emmy. You've never done anything like that before.'

I don't know what the right thing to say is.

'I just want to understand,' says Mum.

I roll the hem of my jumper round and round like a Swiss roll.

'Emmy, talk to me.'

'It was Vanessa. She's the one who said my clothes were ugly, and she calls me a weirdo, and she got her friends to surround me, and they wouldn't let me leave.' I'm blubbing and I don't think anything I'm saying is coming out clearly.

'So this girl has been teasing you?'

I nod.

'Why didn't you tell me, Emmy?'

Because it's embarrassing to be hated, obviously. Mum looks all hurt and disappointed. Just because she's my mum, doesn't mean I want to tell her how the girls at school don't like me.

'Or Miss Monday, you could have told her too.'

'I don't know,' I say. I can hear the sob in my voice and I just want to crush it. This is so unfair, getting told off when I'm not the bully. Why has no one told Vanessa off? Why am I the one in trouble?

Mum sighs. 'How many times has she been mean to you?'

'Almost every day.' The lump in my throat makes it hard to talk.

'For how long?'

'Ever since she came to our school. First, she made friends with Ria, 'cause Ria kept giving her make-up and stuff, but then she decided to be friends with Lila too, only she didn't want to be my friend, she wanted to steal Lila.' I'm crying and I can't make myself stop. 'And at the beginning she was on my table for English, but she didn't like it because she kept saying how I was rubbish at spelling and didn't know how to use semicolons and then Miss Monday told her off for helping me and ever since then she's been extra mean to me.'

It's obvious now. All the times Vanessa said if I could do the dance I could be their friend, or if I got the right clothes I could join in, she wasn't trying to help. She was just finding reasons to leave me out.

Mum finally sits down. 'After work, you're going to tell me everything that Vanessa has said or done. I'll write it in a list and then you can show it to Miss Monday. Yes?'

I nod and sniff. I unwind my jumper all the way

and then wind it back up again.

'And, Emmy.' Mum leans over and strokes my hair. 'Next time she does anything, just walk away. Yeah?'

Islandr Message Boards

Video: Binding the Mulch Queen – NO DAMAGE!!!
Comments continued . . .

Bugnose
Omg seriously? This video is totally faked.

MeowMeow
Bugnose if you knew ANYTHING about Emmentine you'd
know she would NOT fake a video!

IndigoChalice
You're in the presence of a master player and you just won't
admit it

Bugnose
You're all brainwashed. This video is totally fake.
Emmentine is a faker.

Cavedancer
Bugnose, it is against the Islandr message board rules to
make hurtful comments about other Islandr members. If
you break them again, your account will be suspended.
The Islandr Team

Emmentine
thanks for sticking up for me everyone! your the best.

LEVEL UP: EXPERT

FIFTEEN

Jude ambushes me the moment I get to school the next morning. 'Miss Monday's going to announce Geek Gang in assembly. And I've designed some posters.'

While I'm examining Jude's drawings, Vanessa arrives, heroically wearing a plaster over her bruise. I remember the envelope in my pocket with the note for Miss Monday.

'Why *did* you punch Vanessa?' Jude asks, when he notices me looking her way.

I shrug. 'She's always mean to me. She was saying horrible things, and my brother said if I punched her she might stop, but it just got me in trouble instead.' I know I sound cross, and it's not Jude I'm cross at, not really. It's Vanessa and Miss Monday and Mum.

In the classroom, I walk to Miss Monday's desk, gripping the envelope so hard it creases. Inside is a piece of A4 lined paper, the days of the week down one side, and a sentence beside each in Mum's handwriting, to say what Vanessa did. Pretty much what she did. Well, the shortest possible version of what she did.

I hope Miss Monday believes me.

Mum and me read it over this morning and she asked if I was happy with it, and I just nodded because it seemed pointless to say, 'No, you missed out when she asked me a mean question. No, you didn't write down the horrible face she made after she sniffed me.' I'd already told Mum all those details and she decided not to write them. They weren't important enough, she said. They weren't horrible enough.

They felt pretty horrible to me.

I drop the note on Miss Monday's desk and watch in silence as she peels it open, pulls out the lined paper and scans over it. My legs are jiggly, like they want to run away.

'Thank you for this, Emmy,' Miss Monday says once she's finished. 'I'll have a word with Vanessa this morning.' She gives me a small smile. I let out a little breath. Maybe Miss Monday isn't completely horrible.

'Thank you.'

'I thought we'd start Geek Gang on Friday lunchtimes. I'm looking forward to see your superstar mulch-fighting skills in action.'

'Er …' I don't know what to say to a teacher who knows about the mulch. I didn't even know teachers played videogames. But Miss Monday has already moved on. 'Right class, today we're continuing with long division.'

After Maths, Miss Monday asks Vanessa to wait behind. Miss Monday has the note my mum wrote and the class behaviour book out on her desk.

As I reach the door classroom door, Vanessa glares at me. Her eyes look fierce enough to shoot fireballs.

■ ■ ■ ■

Obviously, me and Jude are the first people to reach the computer room on Friday lunchtime.

'Where is everyone? What if no one comes?' asks Jude.

'Then it'll just be the two of us playing video games all lunchtime and it'll be perfect.'

'You don't think anyone's going to come,' he says, wiggling his hands.

'They'll come, Jude, we're just early.' The fire door bangs open and a girl slouches down the corridor. 'See?'

It's Ella-May from the other class in our year. She's very tall and has quite a few spots, which make her look like she could be at secondary school already. 'I'm not late, am I?' she asks.

'Only just,' says Jude.

'You're early,' I tell her. 'We're still waiting for Miss Monday.'

'You've got a blog, haven't you?' asks Jude. 'You post book reviews.'

Ella-May shrugs. 'I guess.'

'That's so cool,' says Jude. Ella-May hunches against the display about Romans on the wall opposite. She looks a bit nervous, but I think I know why. I felt just the same when Jude watched my Mulch Queen video.

After Ella-May, some Year Threes and Fours arrive. One boy is clutching a foam sword. Before long the corridor is crowded with kids telling stories and making sound effects. Then the fire door swings open again and Miss Monday's there. 'Fabulous! Glad you all made it,' she calls, unlocking the computer room door. 'Come in, pull up a stool.'

'Sorry I'm late!' says a girl dashing into the computer room at the last second. I think her name's Semira. She played Cinderella in the last school play and got to sing a solo and she wears her hair in two puffs like mouse ears. She's way too cool for Geek Gang.

'Right, everyone,' says Miss Monday, when we're all inside. The computer room is crammed full. 'Welcome to Geek Gang. Everyone here today is part of an elite band of supergeeks. We're going to trade skills and secrets, and together take the computing world by storm.'

The door squeaks open and Marcus slips inside. I didn't expect him to join Geek Gang!

'So, since we've all got different interests and talents, I thought it would be interesting to do a group project, one where we can all have different roles and learn something new. Does anyone have any ideas?'

A forest of hands shoot up.

'We could review games,' says a Year Four boy with a loud voice.

'Or write game music,' says his friend.

'Or we could make an actual game,' one of the

Year Three girls pipes up.

'What sort of game were you thinking?' asks Miss Monday.

'Oh, um.' The girl looks at her friend who giggles. 'I can't remember.'

'I've got an idea for a game,' says Marcus. 'A tactical war game, elves versus orcs, and you have to train your soldiers, build equipment, research technology ...'

'Interesting.' Miss Monday is writing all our ideas on the whiteboard.

'I want to design characters and stuff,' says Semira. 'Especially the monsters.'

'I want to learn more about coding websites,' says Ella-May.

Jude is straining so hard to stick his hand high in the air he might fall off his stool.

'Jude?'

'We could make a game video. Emmy can show us how, she's an expert. Her video got featured on Islandr and everything.'

Instantly lots of voices shout at once. 'Can we see it?'

'I'm on Islandr too.'

'Can we watch it now?'

Miss Monday holds up her hands. 'Maybe at the end. First we need a project. If we did make a video, what game would it be about?'

'Illusory Isles,' says Jude at once.

'Pet Hotel,' says one of the Year Threes.

'Underfleet,' says Marcus.

'See, we all know about different games, don't we? I think this might be a sticking point,' says Miss Monday.

'It doesn't have to be,' I interrupt, desperate to save Jude's idea. 'What if we all talk about our favourite game. We could talk about whatever we're best at.'

'Our gaming superpower,' adds Semira.

'And someone can do the design and someone else can do the music and we'll need a website to show it off,' I add.

'I like that plan,' says Miss Monday. 'Gaming superpowers. Put your hand up if you agree.' Around the room, hands whoosh into the air. 'That's settled then.'

Miss Monday creates different stations around the room and tells us to think of as many ideas as possible. At the audio station, the loud Year Fours whose names are Harvey and Omar show me a website where you can make your own game music and we mess around with bleeps and buzzes. At the video station, Semira and Ella-May are trying out weird video effects on Semira's phone. They video me in slow-mo then flip me upside-down then turn me lots of weird colours. Even Marcus asks for advice on his superpower, at the content station.

'Does it sound more impressive if I say I'm a guild leader or if I say I'm the master tactician, or something else?'

'I don't know. Jude's really good at words, though. Ask him.'

Marcus nods seriously and goes to find Jude.

Lunchtime seems to vanish, and I can't believe it when Miss Monday says its nearly time for lessons.

'Before we go,' she begins, but she's interrupted.

'Emmy's video!' shouts Semira.

'Yeah, we want to watch the video,' agrees Harvey.

'That's what I was just about to say,' says Miss Monday. She turns on the whiteboard. The video is already loaded, Emmentine frozen mid-dash. Miss Monday hits play.

I don't watch my video. I've seen it so many

times I don't need to.

I watch the people watching it.

The glimmering lights of the stalagmite cave flicker in their eyes. When Emmentine sinks through the fog, they gasp, and when the Mulch Queen swings her arms someone squeals.

Swirling lights and glowing crystals and lashing vines. *Flash, snap,* the last vine clutches the Mulch Queen and the cave cracks open.

'Yes!' yell several voices, and one person says, 'Get in,' which makes everyone laugh.

I can't help it. There's a giant grin all over my face.

As we get up to leave, I can hear everyone chattering about my video. I run to catch up with Jude on the stairs.

'Geek Gang is the best lunchtime club ever,' I say.

'Yeah,' he mumbles, but he doesn't sound convinced.

'I can't believe everyone watched my video. That was so cool.' I wait for Jude to reply, but he doesn't even look at me. 'Jude? Are you alright?'

'Emmy,' He stops suddenly, chewing his lip. 'I don't think I have a gaming superpower.'

IslandrChat

MeowMeow
How do you get the Amber Jewel from the Swamp Duchess?

IndigoChalice
You have to fight her. but if you rescue the traitor steward from the dungeons first he makes the fight easier.

MeowMeow
I didn't think of that.
Wait how do you rescue the steward? there are WAY too many Mulchbugs to fight down there.

IndigoChalice
cackles

Emmentine
GUYS!!!!!!! SPOILERS!!!!!!!!!!!

MeowMeow
OOPS sorry emmentine

SIXTEEN

'Emmy is definitely allowed to come over today, isn't she?' Jude asks his mum as we leave school on Monday. 'I can't play Illusory Isles II without her, I promised.'

'As long as there's no punching.' Sonja gives me a hard look. Mum was on the phone for ages yesterday telling Sonja I'm definitely, absolutely not going to punch Jude like I punched Vanessa.

My face goes hot. 'Obviously not.' The way Sonja looks at me makes me feel like I'm five years old.

Sonja nods, twirls around and leads us to the car. Today she's wearing a puffy skirt covered in flowers and a big-brimmed hat.

'I like your skirt,' I tell her, trying to be nice.

She swishes it this way and that. 'I'm afraid Jude thinks I'm a bit of a show-off.'

'It's annoying,' says Jude, as we climb into the

car, but he sounds as if he's used to it.

'Jude likes to wear quiet clothes, but Jude is a quiet person. I'm a loud person.' And she sings songs at the top of her voice all the way back to the estate to prove it.

As we pull close, I want to slide down in my seat, just in case Vanessa is home and spots me. But I don't. I grip the shiny seat fabric and stare straight ahead. Vanessa won't do anything, not now Miss Monday knows about her.

As we climb out of the car, Jude says, 'I'll make cheesy ham cubes. You can get the game running.'

'Don't go using the sharp knife, Jude!' yells Sonja as he dashes to the kitchen.

Jude's bedroom floor has been tidied since last time. There are new models drying on the desk and one patch of the floor is scattered with pictures of characters from Illusory Isles. There's JadeMage with his plaited beard, the four-armed Mulch Queen, so big she takes up two pages, and lastly a fire elemental with lion claws and a glowing mane—that must be Emmentine!

I hear feet on the stairs and turn on the TV and scrunch down on one of the beanbags. I haven't played Illusory Isles II in five whole days. My skin is fizzing.

Jude clatters in clutching a plate of cheese cubes wrapped in ham. He hands me the plate and picks up the gamepad.

The Illusory Isles II theme tune sparkles from the speakers, bursting over me like a magic wave.

Our SAVE loads with JadeMage standing in the stone circle. We look around at the red, green, and gold tiled floor and collapsed pillars.

'It looks like a temple,' I say.

'A ruined temple,' Jude agrees.

I put the last cheesy ham cube in my mouth as JadeMage investigates the woman tied to a pillar. JadeMage takes the dagger from his belt and swish, the woman is freed. Faded green robes embroidered with flowers fall from her shoulders. Her hair is long and straight and white.

'She looks like a healer,' says Jude.

'Talk to her—perhaps she knows something.'

```
Tia Treekeeper: Thank you, enchanter. It
is so long since I have practised any-
thing but the healing arts that I have
```

forgotten how to fight. But now that the
Mulch Queen has returned to Shade, I fear
we must all be ready for battle.

A list of options appears on the screen:

> I could use the expertise of a healer.
  Will you join me?
> Tell me about the temple.

'Look, we can get a companion!' says Jude.
'But I don't want—' but it's too late. He's
already clicked.

Tia Treekeeper has joined your party!

'What did you do that for?' I ask.
'She can help us,' says Jude. Now, when
JadeMage runs, Tia Treekeeper runs behind.
'But I've never had a companion before.' I'm
watching Jude's hand on the gamepad in case
there are any special controls for Tia. 'When I
play, Emmentine does everything herself.'
Up ahead there's a wide circle of mulchified
ground, but JadeMage skirts around it towards

an encampment of red and purple striped tents.
The camp is full of lights and crackling fires and
music; a troupe of travelling actors crossing the
plains. They tell JadeMage they're packing up to
leave, because they're being chased by maggot-like
creatures, which crawl from the swamp at night.
JadeMage and Tia Treekeeper set off at once to
destroy the maggotty beasts.

'Do you want to try?' Jude holds up the
gamepad.

'I don't know what spells she can do.'

'That's why it's fun.'

I take the gamepad and squidge myself right
down into the beanbag. I press the thumbstick
forward and JadeMage and Tia Treekeeper follow
a dirt trail into the mulchified scrub. JadeMage
holds a lantern against the dark as stars begin to
twinkle overhead.

Suddenly the swampy ground bubbles as
Mulchbeasts burst from below. The maggots are
as big as tree trunks and have rings of sharp teeth.
They wriggle and squirm as they seethe towards
JadeMage and Tia Treekeeper.

'Use Tonic of Might first,' says Jude. JadeMage
grabs a potion and chugs it down. 'That gives a

boost to JadeMage's attacks for the next minute,' Jude explains. 'Now attack!'

I hit the buttons and JadeMage flings a fire potion at the maggots. The bottle bursts into a circle of flames, while JadeMage throws Thunderous Gas. The gust sweeps the Mulchmaggots back and they writhe, their stubby tails squirming.

I'm already getting the next potion ready, when Jude says, 'See if Tia Treekeeper has a shield charm.'

'A what?' The maggots have regrouped and they're getting closer. Any second they're going to plough into the heroes' legs and knock them flying. 'Can't I just blast them?'

'Look! Sphere of Protection!' Jude points to the spell hovering over Tia's head. I hit the button and Tia casts the spell.

A bubble of swirling, purplish air appears around the two heroes and the Mulchmaggots bounce off it, munching at nothing with their saw teeth.

My mouth hangs open. 'I didn't know healers could do that.'

'That's why companions are useful.' Jude looks

particularly smug. The maggots bounce and beat at the circle but they can't get in. JadeMage throws one last bottle, his aim dead on. The maggots fizzle and hiss before exploding into a shower of guts and acid which slides harmlessly off the shield.

'We did it!' I pump my fist. 'We totally did. That shield charm is amazing—no damage from their acid attack! Here.' I hand the controls back. 'That's your superpower sorted. I'm good at the fighting, but you're much better at crafting the right potions and knowing all the spells. That's what makes us a team. Where shall we go next?'

JadeMage and Tia travel across a rickety bridge, through an eerie forest and have just found an intriguing set of caves, when Sonja shouts that it's time to go.

I grab my bookbag and head for the bedroom door.

'Emmy?' I turn. Jude clutches something in his fist. 'Do you want this?' He holds out his cupped hands. Inside, lies a plastic Warsorcery figure shaped a lot like an elemental. Jude's painted the cloak deep reddish-purple and the hair orange. 'It's meant to be Emmentine. Obviously, the face looks a bit different.' The head is more like a bear than a lion, but it's close.

'It's perfect.' I tuck it into my pocket and squeeze it tight.

'We'll always look out for each other, won't we?' Jude says, suddenly sounding all solemn.

'Always,' I promise.

SEVENTEEN

I've never had a friend who's given me a gift they made all by themselves before. I'm in my room, playing with my cardboard islands and new Emmentine model, when there's a knock on my bedroom door. Paul steps inside carrying a present wrapped in sparkly paper.

'What's that?'

'It's a birthday present,' he says.

'Who for?'

'You. Now, I know it's not your birthday for few more weeks. But I have an inkling that you're really looking forward to this present. So, I came to ask if you wanted it early.'

The present is small and rectangular and it's either a book or a DVD or …

Maybe it's Illusory Isles II.

'I think I might want it early,' I whisper.

'If you do open it now, it's important that you

know that this is your biggest birthday present, so you won't have much to open on your actual birthday. And the only reason it's early is because Jay, who I work with, somehow ended up with two copies, so he was selling one on the cheap—'

I hold out my hand for the present and peel off the sparkly paper and it *is* Illusory Isles II. I give Paul a big hug and say, 'Thank you, thank you, thank you,' and run downstairs to the computer.

Before I play it, I have one important thing to do.

Dear Cavedancer

Ive finally got Illusory Isles 2! I hope it isn't to late to do a video bcause I REALLY want to. Ill do it as quickly as possible I promise.

Emmentine

■ ■ ■ ■

In assembly, Mrs Trimble is still banging on about the writing competition.

'I've already received some lovely entries. One about a space explorer, and one about a butterfly who's too scared to fly. Don't forget the deadline is in less than two weeks.'

'Have you written your entry yet?' I ask Jude, when we go out to break.

'What?' Today he's got carrot sticks for his snack. He brandishes one like a tiny orange sword.

'The story competition. I thought you were writing something.' I spot Vanessa, Ria, and Lila on the other side of the playground. I always look out for them now, but they've left me alone since I gave Miss Monday that note.

'I was,' says Jude, swishing the carrot stick about, 'but it wasn't very good, so I stopped.'

'You should finish it. You're the best writer I know.' Jude lunges at an imaginary enemy, acting as if he can't hear me. 'You've still got two weeks to write it.'

'Nothing I write will be good enough to win,' he says, and he bites the end off his carrot stick. 'Anyway, why don't you enter, if it's so important?'

I gape like a fish, but I'm saved from answering by voices behind me.

'You ask her.'

'No, you.'

I spin around. It's those two loud Year Four boys from Geek Gang, acting weirdly shy and giggly.

'Go on.' Harvey pushes Omar forward.

'You were the one in the video, weren't you?' asks Omar. 'The one we watched at Geek Gang? Emmentine.'

I puff up. I feel famous.

'Yeah, that was me.'

'Well, we just wondered . . . Harvey, you ask!'

Harvey pushes in front of Omar. 'We just wondered,' he pauses to bow with a flourish of his hands, 'if it pleases Your Mighty Mulch-Fightyness, if we could add you as a friend on Islandr?' He's kind of pompous, but I don't mind being called *Your Mighty Mulch-Fightyness.*

'It does please me,' I do a queenly wave. 'Tell me what your usernames are next Geek Gang. I'll add you then.'

'See? Told you she'd say yes,' Harvey says, as they rush away.

'That was weird,' I say, turning to Jude, who laughs awkwardly.

'Not really. You've probably got everyone wanting to be your friend now.'

'I'll tell them to add you on Islandr too,' I say, but he just shrugs. 'Oh, and I've got another exciting thing to tell you. Paul gave me my birthday present early, so now I can play Illusory Isles II any time I want.'

Jude's mouth drops open.

'I know, it's so cool. I've already got past the Mulchmaggots, and now I'm exploring the Fae Valley, with the flute trees. Have you got there yet?'

'I've been waiting for you to come over,' says Jude, 'so we could play it together.'

'Well, you don't have to wait any more,' I grin. 'And I can make my video for the Islandr tour after all!'

'Oh,' he says, inspecting his shoes. 'That's really good. I'm glad you get to make your video.'

'I know, I'm so relieved because people on Islandr were asking when the next video would be and I didn't know what to say.'

'What are you going to make it about?' he asks. 'The Mulchbear fight?'

'Someone's done that already,' I say.

'Oh yeah, obviously,' says Jude. 'You'll find something. You're the amazing Emmentine.'

We've walked halfway round the playground now, nearly as far as Vanessa's bench. I almost

144

grab Jude's arm and steer him away, but I don't want to be scared of Vanessa any more, so I keep strolling, chin high.

'Do you really think you'll win, then?' Ria asks Vanessa, as we walk by.

'Well, I once had a poem published in the newspaper where I used to live, so I'm pretty sure.' Vanessa sounds almost bored. 'Like, who exactly at this school could beat me?'

Ria laughs. 'That's so true.'

'Hi Ella-May! Hi Semira!' I say as loud as I can.

They're huddled in the corner of the playground, deep in conversation, but Semira grins as soon as she sees us, and I pull Jude over so he won't hear Vanessa say anything else. She's such a show-off.

'Emmentine!' says Semira. Everyone at Geek Gang calls me that now. 'You both have to tell me your gaming superpowers. I still haven't thought of mine.'

'Jude's is finding all the different potions on Illusory Isles. And mine is beating the Mulch Queen.'

'Oh, of course,' says Semira.

Ella-May rolls her eyes. 'She's just being nice.

It's me who hasn't thought of my superpower yet. Other than losing all my lives in the first five minutes.'

'I told you, that's not a superpower,' says Semira.

'Well, what am I supposed to pick? The only thing I'm good at is writing.'

'Are you entering the writing competition?' Jude asks.

'I am,' Semira interrupts. It's hard to stop Semira from talking. 'But I've got no chance against Ella-May. She's like a professional writer.'

'I just have a blog,' says Ella-May, going red.

'Exactly! Well, I'm going to try anyway. Maybe Jemima Crown secretly loves stories about evil unicorns and exploding sweet factories?'

'Vanessa thinks she's going to win,' I tell them, 'but I think Jude could beat her.'

'Oh, you *so* could,' says Semira, her eyes wide. 'You've got tons of imaginations, Jude.'

'How do you know?' asks Jude.

'Anyone who plays Illusory Isles has a masses of imagination. That's just a known fact.' Semira nods wisely.

'I'll think about it,' says Jude.

'See?' I tell him, as we stroll away. 'Your story is going to blow Jemima Crown's head off.'

EIGHTEEN

On Friday, Jude makes me eat my sandwiches so fast I get stomach ache. After that, we sprint back to the cloakroom to drop off our lunchboxes. 'Now to the computer room,' says Jude, just as Miss Monday walks out of the classroom with a soup can in one hand.

'What are you two up to?'

'Geek Gang's going to start any second.'

'I haven't even had my lunch yet. Go outside for fifteen minutes.'

Miss Monday walks off, swinging her can of soup.

'But she'll have to heat it up in the microwave, and that takes five minutes, and then it'll be too hot to eat for ages—' says Jude, as I lead him onto the playground. I stick my hands in my trouser pockets and rub the elemental model Jude gave me on Friday. I brought it to school to remind me of what

Jude said: we'll always look out for each other.

That means it's my job to distract Jude.

'Have you ever played Superheroes?' I ask. 'Me and Lila used to play it every day. Basically, you pretend the school is under attack from something evil like dragons or aliens ...'

'Or the Mulch Queen?'

'Exactly, but we're superheroes and it's up to us to save the school. But you have to be sneaky so the Mulch Queen doesn't know we're onto her.'

'So, what do we do?'

'First we have to find where the Mulch Queen is and work out her evil plan.'

We search the monkey bars and benches and behind the PE shed, but eventually Jude stops in the middle of the playground.

'Do you sense that? A rumbling from down below?' He's gone into storyteller mode. I can tell because he's putting on a deep, wizardly voice.

'What is it?'

'The Mulch Queen has made her lair very close by. I think... it's in the sewers!'

'The sewers?'

'What's in the sewers?'

I spin on the spot. Vanessa's behind me, shiny

149

black jacket zipped to her neck and a smirk on her face. Ria and Lila stand on either side. My mouth dries up.

'What's in the sewers? Is it your orange trainers? Why aren't you wearing them anyway?' I stare at her, my mouth tight shut. 'Are you going to answer me?'

She knows I'm not. I know how this goes, if you answer, she turns your words into something stinking and slimy and flings them back at you.

Jude doesn't know that rule though.

'We're looking for the Mulch Queen,' he says. 'It's a game we're playing called Superheroes.'

Lila's eyes widen at me, as if I've betrayed her by playing Superheroes with someone else.

'Jude, does Emmy think she's your girlfriend?' asks Vanessa. Lila giggles.

'Oh, gross,' says Ria. 'Emmy and Jude, kissing in a tree, ugly as two freaks can be.'

'Ria!' says Vanessa, grabbing Jude's arm and dragging him close to her. 'Jude isn't an ugly freak. And he's definitely not kissing Emmy. Are you, Jude?'

Jude's face goes purple. He stares at his shoes. 'Well, we're not boyfriend and girlfriend,' he says quietly. My face burns.

'Oh, Jude, don't go there,' says Vanessa. 'Take it from your real friend, Emmy's weird. For one thing, all her clothes are covered in pee.'

Jude clutches the seams of his trousers and looks from Vanessa to Ria. I can't breathe in properly.

'Jude, did you hear what Emmy did to me?' Vanessa nudges him like she's sharing a joke. 'She punched me. Right in the face.' Vanessa touches her cheek gingerly, like it still hurts, even though the bruise is long gone. 'Tell me you're not friends with a meanie like that.'

Jude looks from me to Vanessa and back again. His eyes are wide behind his glasses.

'Go on, Jude.' Vanessa puts an arm around him. 'Say it. Tell me you're not friends with meanies. Meanies who punch people.'

'I'm not friends with meanies,' Jude mutters in the smallest voice possible.

Just walk away, Mum said.

'Make sure Emmy hears, Jude, because she seems to think you're friends,' Vanessa says, but I push past her. I hurry towards the football pitch. I imagine Jude running after me, tapping me on the shoulder to tell me that Vanessa is horrible and he didn't mean what he said.

When I look behind, it's Vanessa, Ria, and Lila who are following.

'Jude!' I shout. He's standing by the wall, twisting his hands together. 'Jude!' His hands freeze. Then he runs into the cloakroom.

Vanessa pulls a face. 'He was never friends with you, Emmy. Accept it.'

I keep walking, round the goalposts and down the side of the pitch. He's going to get a teacher, right? He'll be back any second with Miss Monday. I push my hand in my pocket and grab the Emmentine model.

'Nice one, by the way,' says Vanessa. 'You're the one who punches me, and I'm the one Miss Monday tells off. Good one.'

I wish a football would fly out and smack Vanessa on the head.

'Yeah, good one,' says Ria. 'Vanessa was totally innocent.'

'Yeah, I was.' Vanessa runs to stand in front of me, blocking the path around the football pitch. Ria and Lila are right behind.

Just walk away. I veer across the pitch.

'Hey, where are you going? We're talking to you.'

The footballers don't like it when you spoil their game. One kicks the ball at my ankles and the rest gather in a clump, yelling.

'Get out the way!'

'We're in the middle of a game.'

I push through them, but Vanessa, Ria, and Lila are still close behind.

'Here's the stupidest thing,' Vanessa says. I weave through skipping ropes and handstand competitions. 'Miss Monday actually said I'm bullying Emmy. Bullying!'

'Bullying?' says Lila.

'We're just asking questions,' says Ria. 'How is that bullying?'

I dodge between girls practising a bum-wiggling dance routine and kids snatching each other's football cards.

'It's not like we beat her up,' says Vanessa. 'You should have seen the bullying that happened in my old school. That was real bullying.'

'Yeah, Emmy punched you, not the other way around,' says Ria.

'Exactly, she's the one bullying me.'

I hate them, and they're wrong, they have to be wrong, and I just have to keep walking until Jude comes back with Miss Monday, and why has he disappeared?

I start to run, but Vanessa is faster than me.

'Where are you even going?' Vanessa asks as they catch up.

I'm nearly back at the wall, and Jude still isn't here. I race into the cloakroom and slam the door closed behind me. I glance around the gloomy cloakroom, but there's no sign of Jude. Behind me, the door crashes open, and I sprint towards the girls' toilets.

There's no one inside. Just two empty cubicles and that smell of old pee and chemicals.

I dash into the far cubicle and lock it.

They can't get me now.

Hinges squeal as Vanessa, Ria, and Lila come into the room behind me.

'Emmy, we know you're in here.'

I stare at the cubicle wall with its pattern of criss-crossing lines. Silently, I breathe in through my mouth and out again. In, out. *Thud, thud*, goes my heart against my chest, but I breathe slow, slow. My throat is dry, but I don't dare gulp.

Outside they start to whisper, but no matter how quiet I breathe, my heart is too loud and I can't hear. They giggle, shuffle, shush each other.

If I squint my eyes, the lines on the cubicle wall blur into a smooth blue surface.

Bang. The cubicle door judders. Two hands grasp the top, then Vanessa's head pops up.

'Why are you hiding Emmy?' says Vanessa. 'We're not doing anything.'

My hands shake and I can't make my breathing go slow any more, it rags in and out, and I hate her, I hate her, I hate her, and I'm trapped. What do I do, try and get out?

'Oh, are you upset? What are you upset about?'

'I hate you,' I whisper. My face is crumpled and my eyes are wet. Do I sit on the toilet seat? Just stand here?

Vanessa laughs. 'Sorry, did you say something?'

'I HATE YOU,' I shout, but I shout it at the wall because I don't want to look at her. My face feels like a wet mess and I don't want her to see it.

'Emmy says she wants to go to the toilet,' Vanessa says over her shoulder. 'Well, go on then. We'll make sure no one comes in. Lila, stand by the door.' Feet shuffle outside the cubicle. Now there's no chance of being rescued. 'Go on,' says Vanessa, 'pull down your pants.'

My face drips and drips. I stamp my foot like Pie does when he's angry.

Vanessa giggles. 'Pull down your pants, Emmy. Can't go to the loo in your pants. What a mess.'

'Pull down your pants,' chants Ria, her voice muffled by the door.

'Pull down your pants.' Vanessa joins in. 'Pull down your pants.'

My head feels full and hot and murky and I just stand there, with snot bubbling from my nose and fat tears falling down my cheeks and splatting on the floor.

'Pull down your pants, pull down your pants.'

And I remember the Mulch Queen lurking in the sewers, and I want to sit on the toilet and get sucked down into her lair, because I know how to beat the Mulch Queen, even though she's a four-armed monster with the power to turn things to slime. But I don't know how to beat Vanessa.

And that's so ridiculous that I want to laugh or shout or something, but I just let out a big 'HERGH' instead.

'Oh no, did you poo your pants?' Vanessa is still

leaning over the cubicle door. 'Eurgh, I can smell it. I'll get you something to wipe yourself, shall I?'

'I didn't poo my pants,' I whisper, but Vanessa has already hopped down.

'Lila, give me that.' The door judders again as Vanessa leaps back up. 'Here.' She holds up Lila's cardigan. 'Wipe your bum with this.'

'Hey,' Lila shouts, but too late. Vanessa flings the cardigan and it sails past me, landing half in the toilet.

'Oh. My. God.' Vanessa looks like she's about to burst into hysterics. 'I can't believe you put Lila's cardigan down the toilet, Emmy.'

'Vanessa!' says Lila.

Vanessa ignores her. 'I'm telling Miss Monday what you did.'

What's the point of fighting? Vanessa always wins.

I lean against the wall and slide down onto the floor.

'Come on, we have to go and tell a teacher.'

Vanessa leaps down, Ria shrieks, and one of them opens the door to the cloakroom.

'Come on Lila,' says Vanessa. Silence.

'Come on Lila,' says Ria. Silence.

'Fine, stay there then.'

The door slams closed.

I sit on the toilet floor a moment longer. I can't see the criss-cross pattern on the wall any more. My eyes are too foggy.

Slowly, I stand up. I look down at the cardigan. Half of it is still in the water. Someone has to take it out.

I grab the dry sleeve and pull it from the toilet bowl. Toilet water drips over the floor and I twist my legs out the way. Holding it as far out as I can reach, I unlock the cubicle door.

Lila stares, eyes wide, mouth screwed up like a ball of paper.

'It wasn't me,' I say. 'Vanessa threw it down the toilet, not me.' I hold the dry sleeve out to her.

Lila doesn't take it. Her face creases up. She marches out of the toilets without a word.

I drag the cardigan to the little sink and squash it in. I run both taps and squeeze lots and lots of hand soap on the wool to get it clean.

I don't really want to touch it, so I just leave it there.

Lunch must be nearly over. And Jude just *left* me to go to stupid Geek Gang.

I hate him.

I slowly shuffle back into the toilet cubicle.
Slowly lock the door. Slowly put the lid down on
the toilet. And then I sit down.

I pull the plastic Emmentine model out of my
pocket. Its bristly face snarls at me. *We'll always
look out for each other*, Jude said.

Yeah. Right.

NINETEEN

As I head to school after the weekend, the swamp of mulch rises up to my chest. I know Miss Monday is going to tell me off for putting Lila's cardigan down the toilet. Even though I didn't. And now Jude isn't my friend, and I told Miss Monday about Vanessa like I was supposed to and it just made everything worse.

By the time we do spellings, Miss Monday still hasn't mentioned the cardigan. I stare at my spelling book. My brain is so busy thinking about how I'd like to sink into the mulch and vanish, that I don't hear the words we're meant to spell.

I get two out of ten. Vanessa gets ten out of ten, for the third week in a row. She jumps out of her seat, waving her book in the air and prances off to show Mrs Trimble. When she comes back, she's all swaggery, with a golden sticker on her shirt that says STAR PUPIL.

'Not only is Vanessa a spelling star,' says Miss Monday beckoning Vanessa to stand in front of the whiteboard, 'she's also been working hard on her story for the school writing competition—'

'—judged by Jemima Crown—' Vanessa interrupts.

'—and I thought we could hear a bit of it.'

'I've written eight pages.' Vanessa holds up her glittery notebook—the one she's always writing in—and opens it in the middle.

I thought that book was full of secrets! Is she going to read them out to the whole class? The mulch climbs up to my neck. I look at Ria, who's staring out the window. Lila arranges her gel pens in a pattern on the table. They don't look worried …

'On a starry night, in a small town in England, a girl lived happily with her mum and dad and big sister …

Vanessa reads and reads. I keep waiting for her to say something horrible about me, but it seems to be just a story. A story about a girl a lot like Vanessa, who happens to have magic powers so she can fly and dance on clouds and eat rainbow cake whenever she wants. I can't believe Vanessa's just been using her notebook to write stories in.

At the end, Miss Monday claps her hands. 'Wonderful. Now, does anyone want to say one thing they like and one thing Vanessa could improve?'

Silence.

Then Marcus raises his hand.

'Um? It was boring.'

'Miss, he can't say that,' says Vanessa.

'It just was.' Marcus shrugs. 'I can't help it if I was bored.'

'OK, Marcus, and one thing you liked about it?' asks Miss Monday.

'When it ended?' says Marcus. A few people laugh, even Ria. Vanessa slaps the notebook shut and stomps back to her seat. She's muttering about 'this school' and 'don't know anything.'

'Vanessa, I didn't find it boring,' says Miss Monday, 'but if you like, I can show you how to add some more drama before you hand it in.'

Ugh. Typical Vanessa. Even when she's messed up, she's going to get help from Miss Monday and win the writing competition anyway.

'Who else is writing a story?' asks Miss Monday.

About half the class puts their hands up. Jude raises his fingers, like he doesn't want anyone to see.

'Excellent!' says Miss Monday. 'Don't forget the competition deadline in next Tuesday. You have just over one week.'

Our task in English is to write instructions. 'Instructions for something you do in real life,' Miss Monday explains. 'What sort of thing could you write about?'

'How to make flapjack.'

'How to build a spaceship.'

I wish someone would write How to make Vanessa disappear, so I could read it.

Lila doesn't usually talk much in lessons, but now her hand shoots up.

'How to be a good friend,' she huffs.

'That's a lovely idea,' says Miss Monday. Ria nudges Vanessa and whispers, but Vanessa doesn't react.

'Books out, class. Emmy, Jude, and Marcus, computer room again? Oh, Emmy, wait.'

I stop halfway to the door. The mulch sloshes up to my chin. I know Miss Monday's going to ask about the cardigan.

'We were expecting you at Geek Gang on Friday,' I wait, staring at my feet. 'Jude was really worried about you.' Yeah, right. That's another thing Jude has ruined. Now I can never go to Geek Gang again. 'Is everything alright?'

I shrug.

'Well, I hope you'll join us this week,' she says to my silence. 'We're going to start making videos, we need your expertise. Go and join the others, then.'

I hurry to the door, but when I reach the deserted corridors, I slow down until I'm going slower than a slow walk. Outside the computer room, I wait watching dust float in the sunlight past last term's art displays.

Eventually, I push the computer room door open. Marcus is sitting in his usual place. Jude is sitting in the furthest, gloomiest corner.

Silently, I sit next to the printer by the door.

I open a document and type the title. There's one thing only I know how to do:

How to beat the Mulch Queen with NO DAMAGE

I look over my shoulder. Jude drums on the

desk with his fingers.

Step 1. Go to the cave with all the stalagmites and green fog, which is where the Mulch Queen lives.

'Emmy?'

'Argh!' I almost fall off the stool. Jude has crept up behind me. 'What?'

'I just wanted to say,' Jude takes a shaky breath. He looks all puffy like he might cry. 'I thought we were friends.'

'*I* thought we were friends.' I turn away. 'I'm trying to do my writing.'

'And on Friday, I wanted to go to Geek Gang, but you kept saying to wait.' His voice catches. 'And then you just walked off. You never even turned up.'

I feel cold and hot at the same time. I stare at him. His face is so squashy I just want to squeeze it into a tiny ball and throw it across the room.

'What do you mean—' my voice is shaky too, which is annoying '—I *just walked off*?'

'Vanessa and her friends were talking to you, then you just walked off with them.'

'I didn't walk off *with* them, I was trying to get

away from them.'

Marcus has stopped even pretending to work. He stares over his shoulder.

'Well, why didn't you come to Geek Gang?'

'I thought you went to get *help*. I thought you were coming back.'

'But it was time for Geek Gang to start.' Jude's voice is so thick now it's hard to hear the words. 'Why would I come back?'

'They were horrible to me, Jude. They trapped me in the toilets, and they threw Lila's cardigan in, and said it was me who did it. And Vanessa's *your* friend, apparently.'

'It's not *my* fault,' says Jude, 'I wasn't there.'

'Exactly.' I slam the mouse on the table and pull my stool in as close as it will go.

I try to type, but I can't with Jude sniffling behind me. Eventually, he walks away. *Step 2*, I type, but I can't think what to write next.

I feel in my pocket. The plastic Emmentine model is still there. I take it out and sit it beside the keyboard. Now, that me and Jude aren't friends, I wish I could destroy it.

I could file it to dust with Mum's nail file.

I could twist its head around until it snaps off.

The printer starts to chug beside me. I only see the word **Warsorcery** before Jude snatches the paper. The door slams behind him as he walks out.

The printer chugs again. This time Marcus goes to collect his work.

I haven't written anything!

'Is that a Crimson Archmage of Ceren?' Marcus stops beside my stool, pointing to the model on the counter.

'How would I know?' I'm still typing.

Step 2. Fight the Mulch Queen.

'These are really rare. And really expensive.'

I shrug. 'I don't play Warsorcery. Jude gave it to me.' And then I realize what I'm hearing. Since when does Marcus play Warsorcery?

'It's really well painted.' Marcus brings it right up close to his eye to inspect the details. 'What are you going to do with it?'

'Burn it, probably.'

'No!' Marcus clutches the model in his fist. 'You can't burn the Crimson Archmage of Ceren. Can't I have it?'

I stare. Perhaps this is some sort of trick I don't

understand. Or perhaps Marcus really is an even bigger Warsorcery geek than Jude.

'I've only seen the Archmage for sale in the games shop once, ever, and I couldn't afford it,' he says.

If I give it to him now, I'll never have to think about Jude again.

'Fine,' I say like it's no big deal.

'Yes! Now I have a whole Ceren army. Thanks so much.' Marcus grins and clutches the model. Then he says, 'I liked your video, by the way.'

'My what?' I'm so shocked I add six commas to my instructions by accident.

'Your Islandr video. I don't really play Illusory Isles, but you know how to fight. Have you ever tried Warsorcery?'

'Er …' I delete the extra commas. 'No.' The swamp is sloshing this way and that and I don't know if it's draining away or about to engulf me.

'You'd be good at it,' he says. He leaves the computer room still grinning at his model.

Islandr Message Boards

Video: Binding the Mulch Queen – NO DAMAGE!!!
Comments continued . . .

me55yh3ad
emmentine wen you gonna make anuther video

Lilmisnoface
I was just thinking this—Emmentine is my favourite video maker!

MeowMeow
Emmentine is actually working on something right now. I CAN'T WAIT I'M SO EXCITED

IndigoChalice
In the meantime, why not check out my video commentary of the first hour of Illusory Isles 2?

TWENTY

The hall is always loud at lunchtime but it's not too busy yet. I take my tray with my jacket potato to an empty table. I don't mind sitting on my own, especially not today. I've just got to a tricky bit on Illusory Isles II and I want to think about how to solve it.

The Isle of Shade is shaped like a crescent moon and across the middle are these enormous mountains, the Mordrith. It's completely impossible to go over the top, and the seas either side have been turned to mulch acid which eats up any creatures or boats that try to sail in them. The only way through is the tunnels.

The tunnels are actually a secret city of moon people hiding from the Mulch Queen. To enter from the south you have to find a disguised door and pour an offering of Moonlight Tincture at the shrine. Once you're in, the only way out the other side is through an enormous stone gate. But I don't know how to open the gate.

'Emmentine? Hello?' A hand waves in front of my face. 'Anyone in there?'

'What?'

'You were on another planet,' says Semira. She and Ella-May sit down opposite me and start scoffing their baked potatoes.

'Just thinking about Illusory Isles,' I mutter.

The bit that doesn't make sense is, to open the door you have to spin these two big metal discs at the same time. But the discs are at opposite ends of the mountain. It's impossible. Even if Emmentine spins one and sprints as fast as she can along the quickest path through the twisty caves, even if she avoids getting attacked by Mulchbats, she never gets there in time.

I must be missing something.

'Ella-May gets the same way when she's thinking about her blog,' says Semira. 'Genius at work.'

'You're coming to Geek Gang today, right?' asks Ella-May.

I shrug.

'Oh, you have to come,' says Semira. 'Don't

abandon us.' She tells me everything they did last week, without me. 'And we're supposed to have written scripts so we can film our superpowers today. Oh, that reminds me! I have to get my superpower before Geek Gang starts.' She crams the last of her potato in her mouth,

'*Get* your superpower?' I ask.

'It's a surprise!' says Semira, dragging Ella-May out of the hall.

Maybe I should go to Geek Gang, even if it's just to see Semira's superpower.

I'm just putting my plate away when someone taps me on the shoulder. It's Lila wearing a brand-new cardigan.

'Just so you know, Miss Monday asked me if something happened to my cardie,' Lila says, fiddling with her flowery headband. 'She said Vanessa told her you threw it in the toilet, so I told her Vanessa was lying and nothing happened.'

'Oh,' I say. And then, because I feel like I should say something. 'Thanks.'

'I'm just so sick of her, you know?'

I grunt. I think I am a thousand times sicker of Vanessa than Lila is.

'She told us we weren't even allowed to enter

the writing competition because she's Jemima
Crown's number one fan, so she deserves to win.
Anyway,' she adjusts her headband again, even
though it looks fine, 'I was thinking about signing
up for Geek Gang. You're in Geek Gang, aren't
you?'

'S'pose so,' I say.

'I'll see you there.'

■ ■ ■ ■

I'm nearly the last to arrive at Geek Gang. I'm
pushing my way to the corner furthest from Jude,
when the door slams open. The person in the
doorway is wearing a giant mask that covers their
whole head. It looks like a dragon, with bulging
eyes and razor-sharp teeth.

The dragon struts into the room, lunging at
people who get too close. When the whole of Geek
Gang is captivated, two hands reach up and pull
the mask off.

It's Semira!

'My gaming superpower is … getting inside
the heads of my enemies,' she announces. 'Get it?
Getting inside their heads?' She sticks her head
inside the mask to demonstrate.

Miss Monday puts us in groups to practise our scripts and film together. Omar and Harvey volunteer to help me write my script.

'Can you help Lila too as this is her first Geek Gang?' asks Miss Monday.

As Lila finds a stool nearby, it's like mulch slime creeping towards me across the carpet. I begin to really wish I hadn't come.

Harvey asks Lila what her gaming superpower is, and she thinks for a moment, before saying, 'Definitely something to do with Animal Hotel. I'm obsessed with that game.' She flicks a look at me. 'You remember the time I made you play it, and you decided you'd only play if you could make a reptiles-only hotel?' she asks me.

'Reptiles feel excluded from normal hotels because people think they aren't cute,' I said. We'd made a sunroom and a sand spa and a gourmet insect restaurant for the lizards. 'It was pretty fun actually,' I confess, and the mulch retreats a little.

Miss Monday tapes green backing paper to one wall to use as a green screen. We're meant to stand in front of it to say our lines.

'It won't look like a green piece of paper when we finish editing,' Omar explains. 'We can make it

look like whatever we want using special effects.'
Harvey is already standing in front of it, practising
his lines into a pretend microphone.

I write a few sentences about Illusory Isles
while we wait for our turn to film. I glance at Jude,
who is in a group with some of the younger kids.
He doesn't look like he's having fun.

Well, that's his problem.

We watch Semira deliver her lines in one take,
like she does this kind of thing all the time. Ella-
May mumbles that her superpower is always being
able to recommend a good game, but she has to
film it four times because she talks too quietly to
hear. Then it's my turn.

I've already practised my lines in front of my
group, but somehow it's scarier saying them on
camera.

'I don't think I'll ever be one of those
livestreamers,' I say when I'm done. 'I've got the
shakes, look.'

'No one could tell,' says Lila. 'You looked totally
in control.'

I catch Jude staring at us, but when I meet his
eye he looks away, scowling.

IslandrChat

MeowMeow

EMMENTIIIIIIIIIINE have you done your video yet? I want to SEE IT

Emmentine

Um. I think my version of the game must be broken or something. I can't get past the mountains. Look . . .
mulchbatsareTHEWORST.mp4

IndigoChalice

Haha. I know how you do that bit.

MeowMeow

You have to TELL US. I haven't even got there yet lol. I'm so slow.

IndigoChalice

Nope!!! No spoilers!!!
How long do you have to make your video Emmentine?

MeowMeow

2 days. I reeeally hope I have enugh time.

TWENTY-ONE

'Emmy, can you come out here for a minute?' Mum beckons from the hallway. I'm on Illusory Isles II, getting Emmentine to run around the south half of Shade, just in case there's something I've missed that will get me through the mines.

Mum's holding something behind her back and she looks stern. My stomach wiggles down into my legs. I wrap my arms around myself and shuffle over.

From behind her back, Mum pulls out an orange trainer thick with black paint and a crusty shoelace.

'What happened to your lovely shoes?' My armpits prick. 'Emmy, look at me.' I try to look at her, I really do, but my eyes keep sliding to the wall, the coat rack, the letterbox. 'Do you know why they have paint on them?'

I shrug. Not the right answer.

'They were under your bed, Emmy. I thought

these shoes were what you wanted.'

I sigh. 'I did want them.' My voice is all high
and tight. I take two quick breaths to try to make
the feeling go, but the lump in my throat swells.
'But when I went to school they were the wrong
ones and Vanessa just made more fun of me and
then I thought—' my voice cuts off. The letterbox
is blurry now. 'I thought I could make them better
if I painted over the orange, but it didn't work,
so—'

'So you painted them on purpose?'

I breathe in again, and blink, blink, blink.

'A brand-new pair of trainers. Ruined.'

My eyes are swimming.

'You could have said something, Emmy.'

I look down. Dark tears splodge on the hall rug.

I hear fingernail-scraping sounds, and flakes of
black paint flutter past my eyes.

'I think we can fix this,' Mum says gently.

I nod, take in a long rattling breath and let it
out again. I look at Mum's arms. It's the closest
I can get to looking at her properly. Both are
covered in tattoos, but her left inner forearm is my
favourite, a howling wolf silhouetted against a blue
and purple sky.

'Go and get the other trainer. I'll sort this black paint out.'

I run upstairs, crawl under the bed and grab my other shoe.

In the kitchen, Paul runs my trainer under the tap while Mum spreads old newspaper on the table. Her art box is on the chair. The kitchen feels cosy, just like rainy Sundays in the old days, when we did art projects together, except that today the sun gleams through the open window and there's a friendly buzz of lawn mowers.

'Would you like to apologize to Paul, Emmy?'

'I'm sorry, Paul,' I whisper, placing my other trainer on the table.

'That's OK, Emmy. I know school has been tough. Anyway, your mum has a brilliant idea for how to fix it.'

'Actually, I got the idea from Emmy,' says Mum. 'I was thinking that no one else in the whole school will have amazing customized trainers. We can use Sharpies, ribbons, and gem stones. Sound like a plan?'

'Sounds awesome.' I grin.

'You have a think about how you want them to look.'

I think about the first time I wore the trainers, and how they had the magic power of Megaspeed. What would magic speedy trainers look like?

'Shiny,' I say. 'With loads of gemstones.'

Mum nods. 'Volcanic trainers erupting jewels from the bowels of the Earth,' she says. Mum's artist brain always turns ordinary sounding ideas into something magic.

'Do you want your jacket to match?' Paul asks. Mum gives him a look. 'I can sew, you know.'

I run to fetch my jacket, and when I come back, Mum is drawing flames on the sides of my trainers with marker pens. I pick out silver gems and gold, red, purple, and pink. Some are big diamonds or tiny circles or stars. Paul fetches an old grey shirt, cuts out chunks and paints them the colour of flames.

Then the doorbell buzzes. 'Visitors!' Mum opens the door.

'Hello!' It's Sonja's voice. 'Is Emmy in? Jude was wondering if he could have a chat with her.'

'Of course,' says Mum. 'Emmy, Jude's here!'

I freeze. Paul looks at me. I shake my head and he frowns.

'Jude just wants to apologize. He didn't mean it,

did you Jude?' Sonja adds.

'Didn't mean what?' says Mum. 'Emmy, are you coming?'

'Emmy?' says Paul quietly. 'What's up?'

'Perhaps Emmy didn't tell you,' Sonja continues, 'but she and Jude fell out last week. I was wondering why Emmy seemed to be avoiding us. But I handcuffed Jude to his beanbag and tickled him with a feather, and eventually he told me everything. Jude realizes now that Emmy didn't miss Geek Gang on purpose, don't you Jude?'

'Come on,' Paul says in the quietest voice ever. 'Let him apologize, and then if you still don't want him here, we can ask him to go.' He stands up. 'Need me to hold your hand?'

I'm way too old for hand-holding, but before I can say no, or drop my handful of gems, Paul has wrapped his big square hand around mine.

He leads me towards the door.

'Hi, Jude,' I whisper.

'Hi, Emmy,' Jude whispers back.

'Go on,' says Sonja. Today her hair, lipstick, and summer dress are all the same shade of dark red.

Jude shuffles. 'I'm sorry I was cross you missed Geek Gang. I know you didn't do it on purpose.

And I should have helped when Vanessa was being horrible. She's the mean one, not you.'

Sonja pats him on the shoulder. 'My good boy.' He blinks behind his glasses. Paul squeezes my hand, and it's nice, except for the gems digging into my palm.

'Vanessa's mum works at the bank with Jude's dad, so they're over a lot,' says Sonja. 'Vanessa's been unsettled ever since they moved, apparently. Her old school was quite different, and I don't think she's made any very close friends here, not like her old ones. She misses them.'

'That doesn't make it OK to be mean, Mum,' says Jude, suddenly cross, and all at once I know I'm going to forgive him.

'Of course not,' says Sonja. 'I think she feels a bit out-of-place, that's all.'

Vanessa feels out-of-place? What about me? She was the one who stole my best friend.

Paul clears his throat. 'Now, Emmy, do you accept Jude's apology?'

I nod and smile and Jude smiles back.

'Well, Jude,' says Paul. 'Do you want to come in?'

'Yes, please.'

'More importantly,' says Mum, 'do you like art?'

'Jude is amazing at art,' I say. 'And writing. There's a story competition at school, and the deadline is on Tuesday, and Jude's going to win, I bet.'

'I'm OK at painting models,' Jude admits. 'Not writing though. I couldn't write anything good enough for the competition. What happened to your trainers?'

He has to enter, or Vanessa will win! This is typical of Jude. He needs someone like me to stop him from deleting everything he writes, just like in English lessons. The question is how? The deadline is only two days away.

Mum has already led Jude to the kitchen. 'We're turning them into Megaspeed volcano trainers,' explains Mum, handing Jude a trainer with flame outlines drawn on each side. Jude grabs the permanent markers and draws overlapping lines of red and yellow and orange so the flames look real.

'Hey, Jude, you want to come work in my tattoo parlour?' Mum asks, inspecting his work. 'More talent than some of my apprentices. You can colour the other trainer too, if you like. I'll find snacks.'

'Shall I fetch Ryan?' asks Paul. 'We don't want

him missing out on snacks.'

'Oh, I don't know,' says Mum, digging out the chocolate biscuits. 'Ryan's probably too busy doing teenager things to want to join our little party.' It's true. Ryan does spend most of his time in his room these days.

'Have you finished your Islandr video, yet?' asks Jude, adding orange sparks.

'No, not yet.'

'Oh, I thought you'd have done it by now. I wanted to watch it.'

My stomach wobbles, but if there's anyone I can tell, it's Jude. 'Actually, I'm stuck. I've got to the Caverns of Mordrith but I don't know how to open the gate and reach the north of the island.'

Jude goggles at me. 'You're stuck *there*?' I nod. 'Even I can do that bit. When do you have to make the video by?'

'Tomorrow.' What if I don't make my video in time?

'That's so soon! What companions have you got?'

'Erm.' My insides feel like stones.

Jude puts down his paintbrush. 'You haven't got any, have you? First you need to get some.'

'Can I just come over and see how you did it?'

Jude grins. 'Of course you can.'

While Jude paints, Paul clicks on the radio and sings along in a high-pitched voice that makes Jude giggle and Mum groan. Soon, my jacket has sparks and fireballs busting all over it. Mum plaits pink and orange ribbons into the new laces.

'No one will mess with you in these,' Mum tells me.

'Don't go making me far-ar-art,' sings Paul over the radio, getting the words wrong on purpose. Jude snorts and nearly smudges my shoe, and Mum says, 'Paul, you're such a child.'

That's when Ryan emerges from his room with a maths textbook. 'Mum, can you help me with this? Wait, what are you lot up to?'

'Clothes customization,' says Mum. 'Emmy wanted to upgrade her trainers to superhero trainers.'

'Who's he?' Ryan points at Jude.

'That's Jude, from school.'

'And,' Ryan says at last, 'you didn't think I might want to join in? You just decided to have a nice time making stuff together, without me?'

Ryan looks around at us, and no one says a

thing. The song tinkles on in the background, but all I can hear is, 'Don't go making me far-ar-art,' in my head. I almost giggle, but I clamp my hand over my mouth in time.

'Ryan, I didn't think you'd want to. Actually, Paul said—' Mum starts, but Ryan cuts her off.

'I don't care what Paul said.' Ryan throws his textbook on the kitchen floor with a loud bang. 'Ever since he came along it's like I'm not even part of this family.' And he stomps down the hall, throws open the front door, and strides out into the street.

TWENTY-
TWO

Ryan hasn't come out of his room since he got back
last night. After he marched out, Paul drove after
him, crawling around the block to make sure he
came home. Ryan nearly threw the front door off
its hinges when he barged into the house. His hair
and T-shirt were sopping with sweat and his face
was red and patchy.

'I hate all of you,' Ryan yelled. 'First, you don't
want me involved, then when I try to get some
space you can't leave me in peace.' He shut himself
in his bedroom and jammed the door.

At breakfast, my trainers sit on the table in the
place where Ryan usually sits. The light catches
the gemstones, which cast tiny rainbows across the
table. My jacket hangs from the chair, black and
orange and gold.

'Are you going to wear them today?' Mum asks.
'Show them off?'

I run my fingers over the gemstones. I
imagine wearing them on the playground,
showing everyone who I really am. They'll see
I'm a superhero, the sort of person who can shoot
lightning from my hand, who can make volcanoes
erupt by stomping, who can run like a hurricane.

I'm going to do it.

But what about Vanessa? She'll take one look at
my fire jacket and volcano shoes and ruin them in a
sentence.

'I don't think the glue is dry yet,' I say. 'Maybe
tomorrow.'

■ ■ ■ ■

'I just don't understand how you've got stuck *there*,'
says Jude. We're sprawled on his beanbags after
school, eating cheesy ham cubes. 'All you have to do
is unlock both locks at the same time.'

Jude's bedroom is even messier than normal,
with sheets of paper all over the place.

'Is this your story for the competition?' I ask,
picking one up.

'No,' says Jude, grabbing the paper before I can
read it. 'I haven't written a story.'

'But the competition ends tomorrow.'

'Nothing I write is good enough. Anyway, I'm too busy helping you with your video.'

Illusory Isles II is on the screen and Jude takes the controls. I'm trying not to look, because JadeMage is in part of the map I haven't unlocked and I don't want to see any spoilers.

'It's impossible,' I say. 'Emmentine can't run from one gate to the other in time. And then there's the Mulchbats ...'

'That's what companions are for.' Now JadeMage zigzags through the Caverns of Mordrith. Tia Treekeeper follows behind, along with a moon fairy with skin like the night sky, a ranger with a bow and arrow, and an enchanter with an enormous leather-bound book.

'I don't have any companions. Emmentine can do all the fights on her own.' I stuff the last cheesy ham cube in my mouth.

'Yeah, so far,' says Jude, as the companions enter the caves and face the unmoving stone gate, 'but you just wait. Now, watch.' Jude selects the fairy, Ilva of the Moon, and sends her running up the left path. He selects Tia Treekeeper, who runs up the right path. The remaining companions wait by the gate, spells ready. 'Are you watching?' Jude's fingers hover over the buttons. 'Now!'

Ilva of the Moon yanks the left disc, Tia
Treekeeper spins the right disc. The gates crunch
open and a shaft of light falls on the waiting
heroes. Before they can dash for the gates, the
shrieking Mulchbats descend. JadeMage, the
ranger, and the enchanter are ready, smashing
potions and chanting spells and shooting arrows
and in no time the bats are soup. The heroes run
for the gates and make it onto the mountainside
with seconds to spare.

I'm leaning forward, mouth hanging open.
'That was awesome.'

Jude shrugs. 'It's not that hard once you know
how.'

'But where did you get all those companions?
I've only met Tia Treekeper.'

'I don't mind showing you,' says Jude. 'But don't
forget where they are. Or you won't get your video
finished tonight. Maybe you should draw a map.'

I roll over on my beanbag and grab the nearest
sheet of paper and dig a pencil out from under his
Warsorcery models.

Ilva of the Moon lives in the underground
city near the gate. After that, JadeMage travels to

a collection of camouflaged treehouses, which is
where the ranger, Mal Shatterbolt lives. Finally
JadeMage runs off to a library in a mulch-infested
village where the enchanter, Roghod Humph,
boasts the best spell books but no patrons.

'Have you got everything?' asks Jude, dropping
the gamepad. I show him the map. 'You should go
home if you're going to have time to make your
video.'

Even though I'm not stuck any more, my
insides feel all tight.

'Jude, I still don't know what to make my video
about.'

Jude raises his eyebrows. 'You're the amazing
Emmentine! The Illusory Isles bow before you!
No one defeats Mulchbeasts with the speed
and accuracy you command!' He's doing his
storytelling voice, which makes it all sound super
impressive.

'What if I'm not amazing any more?'

Jude flings his arms wide in despair. 'What do
you mean?'

'I couldn't even work out how to get out of the
cave by myself. You're the one who did that. You're
the amazing player now.'

Jude actually starts pacing about.

'No, I'm not. I'm no good at anything cool or important. Not like you. You can do all the hard stuff, the dodging and running and casting spells. I just get scared and do nothing. It's the same at school. I'm rubbish at everything.'

'No—you're a really good writer. Miss Monday said your story was amazing.'

He gives me a look that makes me want to shrivel up. 'Emmy, she was just saying that to make me feel better. I'm the worst writer in the class. It's a well-known fact.'

'You're not,' I say. 'I'm worse than you.'

'Great, so we're both bad writers.'

'No, that's not what I meant—'

'So, why do I get singled out with you and Marcus to do my writing on a computer then?' he says.

And I don't know the answer to that.

'I'll get Mum to take you home now,' Jude says in a much quieter voice.

As he trudges downstairs, I fold my map to put in my bag. There's something on the back written in Jude's neat handwriting.

On the island of mists and mountains, near the lake of crystal water, lived a hero known as JadeMage. The wise mage, who was sage and learned, was preparing peace potions in his study when a messenger arrived in a flurry of leaves.

'Come quickly! We need your help beyond the mountain!'

But JadeMage would not leave without Emmentine the Brave, for she was the fearsomest fighter in all the land, and she fought with claws of flame...

Jude was lying. He *did* write a story for the competition! And it's about him and me—or our superhero selves anyway.

I reach around the carpet, grabbing all the pieces of paper I can. Jude's feet thud on the stairs as I stuff the pages in my school bag. I pull up the zip as the bedroom door bursts open.

'Mum's waiting,' he says. 'I hope you think of something for your video.'

'Thanks. See you tomorrow.'

Jude is a better writer than he thinks. And now I know how to prove it.

■ ■ ■ ■

When I get home, I shove everything on my
bedroom floor to one side. I tip all the papers I
took from Jude's bedroom out onto the carpet.

Blood beats in my palms. I wonder if Jude
knows his story is missing. I need to hurry. I don't
know if I'll have time to make my Islandr video
too.

But Jude's story comes first. I can already
picture the summer fayre. Jemima Crown, probably
with shiny blonde hair and sunglasses, announcing
the competition winner. It's Jude! He's won! As
everyone cheers, he bounds up the stage, his face
all puffy with happiness. Vanessa stomps about in a
rage because she was sure it would be her.

Piecing together Jude's story is a bit like
solving a puzzle. I sort the papers into neat piles
like clues. Some of the papers I grabbed are bits
of homework or half-finished drawings, but
eventually I have five pages of story lined up in the
right order. I read the whole thing on my elbows
and knees, my hair hanging low enough to swish
on the carpet.

The story is all about how Emmentine and
JadeMage travel far across the island to a place

full of big green trees and giant flowers and happy
people. In fact, they're too happy, as if they've
been put under a spell. I've just got to the bit
where the heroes discover it was a new trick of the
Mulch Queen's to enslave the land, when I realize
something: Jude never wrote the ending.

I gaze at Jude's neat, curly handwriting,
my heart sinking into my knees. I could shove
everything under the bed and forget about it. If
I'm super speedy I can probably still find all the
companions Emmentine needs, get out of the
mountain and make a video before the deadline.

But Jude is my friend. When I just had friends
online, all I wanted to do was make gaming videos
to make them happy. But now I have a real-life
friend, I want to make him happy too. Winning
the story competition will show Jude that Miss
Monday wasn't lying, he really is a good writer.
Better than Vanessa, even.

I'll have to write the ending myself.

I grab the pile of papers and rush downstairs
to the living room. As I push open the door, I hear
familiar rushing and crashing noises, all mixed up
with chanting as if someone is saying a spell.

Ryan is playing Illusory Isles.

'Ryan!'

'What?'

'What are you doing?'

'I'm trying to work out how to beat this Mulchworm.'

'Mulchworm?'

'I've made an enchanter, right, and he has this spell book, but my most powerful spell just bounces off the worm.' He's playing the original Illusory Isles game. His blue-robed enchanter dodges a writhing worm with hundreds of gnashing teeth. 'I'm using Rain of Blades, but the blades don't even dent it.'

'That's because Mulchworms have resistance to slashing attacks.' The worm makes a lunge for Ryan's enchanter. Ryan selects the Icy Bolt spell. A roaring white pillar slams into the worm from above and the worm explodes, splattering green slime.

'Yes! Take that you overgrown fish bait.'

'Ryan, I need the computer.'

I think I sound upset because he spins around.

'When?'

'Right now.'

He exits the game. Just like that.

'What is it?'

It takes a little while to explain about the story competition and how Jude thinks he's no good at writing and how I found his half-finished story in his bedroom. When I've finished, I'm gripping the sheets so hard they've creased.

'Are you sure this is a good idea?' Ryan asks. 'Maybe Jude doesn't want a load of grown-ups judging his writing.'

'No, this will prove he's good once and for all. I *know* it will.'

Ryan frowns, then shrugs. 'You read, I'll type.'

Mum makes dinner. It's pizza-on-our-laps, which is perfect because it means we can keep typing. An hour later, the story is nearly finished. I just need to invent a good ending.

'*When Emmentine and JadeMage got back to the village, the villagers had an awesome surprise for them,*' I say through a mouth of ham and pineapple.

'No, you need to say something like *Emmentine the stout-hearted and JadeMage the level-headed.* That's the way Jude always writes.'

'Er, OK.'

'And I don't think *awesome* sounds right either. What about *glorious*?' Ryan changes the words on the screen.

'*They threw a big party, with cake and pizza, because the slippery slime was gone and the—er—*'

'Sinister?'

'*—sinister mist had vanished. The mystery was solved, and all was well.*' I finish.

Ryan clicks print. 'I'll get you a folder to keep it in,' he says, disappearing to his room.

While he's gone, Mum comes in yawning. 'Have you finished your pizza? It's nearly time for bed.'

'Almost.' I stuff the last piece in my mouth. The cheese has gone cold and chewy.

'Has Ryan been hogging that computer all evening?' Mum says. 'Honestly, that boy never does a thing to help.'

The words come out of her mouth just as Ryan comes back with a cardboard folder. I gulp down my pizza. 'No, Mum—' I say, but I'm not quick enough. Ryan chucks the folder on the sofa and stomps to his room. The door slams so hard the house rattles.

Mum rolls her eyes. 'Don't you ever be that moody, Emmy.'

I have to say something. 'But Ryan *does* help.' I hold my breath. Mum gives me a dagger look. 'He tries, anyway, but when he does, you don't notice. Or you tell him he's wrong. Or Paul says he'll do it instead.'

Mum huffs. 'Paul's just trying to help too. Ryan never sees it.'

'Exactly.'

Mum rubs her hands up and down her forearm tattoos, thinking. Then she says. 'Bed time, Emmy.'

'I just have to send one message.'

'One message, then.' Mum slinks out of the living room. Then she knocks on Ryan's bedroom door and asks to come in.

Dear Cavedancer

I really ergently had to do something for my friend at school. Well it's a long story but I swear ill do a video tomorrow, pretty pleeeeease????

Emmentine

I wipe my cheese-greasy hands on my school trousers, then I carefully pick up the printed pages and put them into the folder. At least I finished Jude's story in time.

TWENTY-THREE

There are lots of people outside Mrs Trimble's office on Friday morning, milling beside the purple post box where we're supposed to post our competition entries. Two girls clutch lined paper covered in horse drawings. A boy puts a whole exercise book through the slot. Ella-May from Geek Gang posts several sheets, handwritten in fancy ink.

I try to push my way through but I keep getting stuck behind people.

Then Vanessa arrives, waving page after page of small neat writing. 'Get out my way,' she says, and the crowd parts for her.

I begin to wonder if Jude has even the tiniest chance of winning. Maybe this was all a mistake.

'Emmy,' Miss Monday is right behind me. 'I'm glad to see you're entering the competition. Here, pass me your story, I'll pop it in for you.'

'It's not my—'

But Miss Monday has already taken the blue folder from my outstretched hand. The folder slips into the box and it's gone.

When I get to the classroom, Jude bounds up to me. I freeze, terrified he knows.

'Did you finish your video for Islandr?' He drags me to our table for English.

'Er—' The truth scrabbles in my mouth, but I won't let it out. 'Yeah. It's even more epic than the last one. But Cavedancer won't be putting it up for a while.'

'Tell me when.' Jude's voice drops to a whisper as Miss Monday asks for quiet. 'We can watch it at Geek Gang.'

■ ■ ■ ■

Sorry Emmentine. The deadline for the video was Monday night. Maybe next time.

Cavedancer

The message is already there when I get home from school. I read it three times. Then I slam my fingers on the keyboard so the screen fills with gobbledegook.

I want to tell someone, but no one at home cares and Jude can't know. So I open IslandrChat and confess everything to MeowMeow.

MeowMeow

NO WAY. It CAN'T be too late. Have you asked for more time?

Emmentine

Cavedancer said no. And now I just don't feel like playing any more. Whats the point if im not making a video?

MeowMeow

That's RIDICULUS! You CAN'T quit!

Emmentine

What if I play it and all I can think about is how Im a failure?

MeowMeow

But you're NOT a failure. You're one of the only people I can talk to about games (you and Indigo) and you always help me out when I get stuck (which is all the time haha).

You could be friends with anyone, after your video got famous, but you're still hanging out with me.

Emmentine
Of course Im hanging out with you! youre the nicest person I know!

MeowMeow
I just don't see why people fight all the time over who's best. It doesn't matter if some people are better than others.

Emmentine
Hm. Maybe I should just play Illusory Isles because its fun.

MeowMeow
YES SO FUN

MeowMeow's right. The reason I love Illusory Isles isn't making videos, it's because it's the best game ever.

As soon as Illusory Isles II loads, I head south of the mountains to find companions. I'm not used to playing with companions, so at first I keep getting things wrong. Like Ilva of the Moon has a spell called Bounding Light, where moonbeams rain down, but if you're not careful they strike the heroes as well as the baddies. Also I keep forgetting Tia Treekeper has healing powers. But Roghod Humph is epic. He has this great scroll spell that makes Mulchbeasts evaporate.

I spend almost the entire rest of the week playing. Emmentine explores the Spiral Forest and the Clockwork Keep and travels with the amphibious People of the Swamp. She finds rare items—a Fleetfoot Necklace, a Scarf of Persuasion—and fulfils quests. When I close my eyes to sleep, I see Emmentine casting Flame Tornado and Sweltering Orb.

■ ■ ■ ■

'Ria, you know the story competition?' Vanessa says, as we file out of the classroom at break time on Friday. As I push through the cloakroom with Jude, we end up stuck behind her and Ria. 'You know how the winner gets their story published?' she continues.

I didn't know that! I shuffle closer, head

ducked, listening.

'Honestly?' says Ria.

'Yeah, they're actually going to make my
story into a whole book. With my name on the
cover?'

'Ugh,' I say before I can stop myself. I hate it
when Vanessa talks as if she's already won the
competition.

What if she has?

'I didn't actually ask your opinion.' Vanessa
turns so suddenly I nearly walk into her. She
pushes her face right up to mine. I try to step
back, but there are too many people behind me.
Jude tugs on my sleeve, but I know walking away
doesn't work, it just means Vanessa climbs up
the toilet door so you can't escape.

I should have kept quiet.

'I didn't say anything,' I mutter.

'Don't lie, you said *ugh*. Are you going to
explain?'

I don't want to explain. I can't explain,
because it's Vanessa, and I know whatever I say
she'll just turn it into something else.

Ria smirks. All around us, people shove,
wanting to get outside. I have to keep my legs

as stiff as possible, so I don't get knocked into
Vanessa.

'You're just jealous of me, aren't you?' says
Vanessa. 'Because I'm cleverer than you and I've
got real friends. You might think you've made
friends, but they're loners who are so desperate
they'd be friends with anyone.' She gives Jude a
look so mean that his chin wobbles.

I should say something. Like *Shut up*, or *Don't
say things like that*, or *It's not true*. It can't be true.

I gulp. What if it is?

'And the only way either of you could win the
story writing competition is if there was a prize
for the worst writer in the school. I'm only telling
the truth, there's no need to get upset.'

I'm not upset. I've made my face completely
blank, like a robot with no feelings. Jude looks as
if he might cry though.

As Vanessa pulls Ria outside, Ria says, 'When
you get published, can I do the cover design?'

'Vanessa was just being horrible, Jude,' I
mutter.

'It's OK,' says Jude, pulling at his face like he
wants to stretch the wobbles out. 'How far have
you got on Illusory Isles?' I think he's trying to

change the subject.

'I'm at the end, nearly.'

'Already?'

'I'll probably finish it tomorrow, before the fayre. You can come over if you like.'

Jude nods slowly. 'Maybe I'll get some tips on how to beat the final boss.'

Vanessa can't win the writing competition on Sunday. She just can't.

IslandrChat

Emmentine
Evryone meet my real life friend...... JadeMage!

JadeMage
Hello! Emmentine has told me all about you.

IndigoChalice
Hiiiii JadeMage!
Have you guys got into the fortress yet?

Emmentine
Only got 2 sidequests to go then FORTRESS TIME

MeowMeow
OMG NO. I tried to get in the fortress but theres no way in
Now Im helping the king of the purple palace avenge his
sister. Only I have to get through this maze and I dont know
how. UGH

JadeMage
The maze is easy, just follow the golden runes.

MeowMeow
I CANT BELIEVE I MISSED THAT. Thanks JadeMage.

TWENTY-
FOUR

The Mulch Queen's fortress: from the outside, the rock is carved into monstrous shapes, giant toads and scaly birds, and insects with a thousand eyes. The walls are too steep to climb and the stone doors are too heavy to budge.

Emmentine's party reaches the fortress by Saturday lunchtime. I munch my bacon sandwiches with extra barbecue sauce sitting at the computer, staring at the fortress walls. In front of Emmentine is a giant lever. She only has to pull it, and her party will battle the Mulch Queen herself.

I hit pause and message Jude to come over, just like I promised.

JadeMage

I AM ON MY WAY DON'T DO ANYTHING TILL I GET THERE.

I pace around the house. Mum is in the kitchen sorting fake tattoos and face paints for the summer fayre tomorrow.

'Emmy! You've dragged yourself away from that game. You're not sick, are you?'

'No, Jude is coming over. I've just reached the Mulch Queen's fortress and he wants to see the final battle.'

'Oh, right.' She snaps a rubber band around a stack of unicorn tattoos. 'You've picked the right day to invite Jude, anyway. Paul's gone out to buy the ingredients for chocolate cake.'

'Yesss! I love Paul's chocolate cake. He's much better at baking than you.'

'Hey!' says Mum, pretend-slapping my arm. She puts three more stacks of tattoos into the box. 'Emmy, you like Paul, right?'

'Of course. Why wouldn't I?'

'And you don't mind him living with us?' She's not looking at me.

'Mind?' I pull a face. 'Why would I mind? He bakes cakes and lasagne and he knows about computer games.'

'Good.' She picks up a pile of animal tattoos and thumbs through them. 'Good. I wish I knew why it bothered Ryan so much.' Her voice is very quiet.

'Um.' It seems like ages ago that Ryan was in my bedroom, cleaning black paint from the carpet. 'Ryan thinks it'll be like Dad all over again.'

Mum's eyes go wide. 'He's not like that, is he?'

'No! Paul makes you happy, not sad. And he joins in with everything.'

'But Ryan doesn't,' says Mum. She's finished putting the tattoos in piles now. 'And he's always sniping at Paul.'

'Sometimes Ryan acts mean to be friendly, though,' I point out. Just then the doorbell buzzes. 'That's Jude!' I run to the door and yank it open. 'I've had the game on pause since I messaged you.'

Jude is already in the hall, kicking off his shoes, even though we don't have that rule. 'I can't believe you've got into the fortress already. I think you've even beaten IndigoChalice.' I drag him by the sleeve into the living room.

The curtains are half-drawn and the computer table is littered with empty cups and chocolate bar wrappers. My blanket is piled on the seat, and there's paper all over the desk. Some of it is Ryan's homework—but some of it is Jude's story.

I dash in, fold up the papers and shove them in the desk drawer. Jude can't see that I took it. After all, it's meant to be a surprise when he wins. Which he will.

Jude's only been to my house once before, when he decorated my trainers. 'We only have one chair,' I say. 'Whoever's not on controls has to sit on the sofa arm.'

'Got it,' says Jude, perching on the sofa.

I sit, adjust my wrists on the table, and tap my fingers on each of the important keys.

'Are you going to video it?' asks Jude.

My stomach squidges. 'But what if I don't do very well? I don't usually do videos until I can do the fight perfectly.'

Jude shrugs. 'Just in case.'

'OK.' I'm still not sure, but I tap the keyboard shortcut so it starts recording. 'Ready?'

'Ready.'

I unpause the game.

The camera swoops through a tunnel of flaming green torches, into an open-air arena full of many-eyed insects, scaly birds, and an enormous drooling toad-dragon. On a throne overlooking the beasts sits the Mulch Queen. She leers, raises her four arms, and bolts of green gunge shoot from her fingers.

'That's so awesome,' I say as the cut-scene ends. Already I'm planning my attack.

'Oh no,' says Jude. 'You should stop the video. You'll never win.'

'Yes, I will. You said I had to video it, so now I have to win.'

Emmentine's purple cloak swishes as she strides through the open doors and down the tunnel, her mane alight with tiny flames. Tia Treekeeper paces forward, Ilva floats on moonlight, Roghod Humph thumps his staff and Mal Shatterbolt stalks in the shadows. Up ahead there's daylight.

The heroes walk out into an arena like a huge stone bowl. An audience of Mulchbeasts buzz and hiss and gurgle. The Mulch Queen watches from her throne, licking her green lips with a long, pointed tongue.

```
Mulch Queen: You fools. You've fallen
right into my trap. My spell is nearly
```

fully charged, and now that I've lured
you to my fortress, you'll never escape
alive. HAHAHA!

Evil laughter echoes around the arena. I gulp.
'You're doomed,' says Jude gloomily.
'I'm not. You'll see.'
A quick scan of the arena reveals four spell
crystals, in niches in the walls.
'I bet we can turn her spell round on her, just
like in the last game,' I say. The heroes run for the
spell crystals, but before they can reach them the
air buzzes. A swarm of many-eyed insects pour
into the arena from every direction. They waggle
furry, jointed legs and snap their pincers. Ilva of
the Moon blasts them with searing moon rays,
Roghod Humph chants a petrification spell and
Mal Shatterbolt fires poison arrows.
Jude keeps yelling advice. 'Aim at the big one.
Do a sweeping attack. Fling it—fling it!' —then
putting his hands over his glasses so he can't see
me do it. Tia Treekeeper throws up Enfeebling
Barriers while Emmentine sweeps with her claws.
But the insects seem to resist almost everything.
The heroes have almost no health by the time a

lucky arrow finishes the last locust off.

'You did it.' Jude stares. 'I can't believe you did it.'

I wiggle my cramping hands. 'See?'

The front door swings open as Paul comes home from buying cake ingredients. 'Hi kiddos!' he calls.

'Hi!'

'Emmy, watch out—' Jude points.

Slash, a talon grazes Emmentine's side. Above, a flock of vulture-like birds soar and squawk. Their necks sag, and their beaks glint like steel.

One hovers and *whoosh,* dives at Tia, who raises a shield spell just in time. Ilva barely dodges as one swipes at her head, and when Mal aims at the nearest bird it emits a raucous enfeebling screech. Mal's arrow misses by miles and hits Tia instead.

'Nooo,' Jude groans.

'What's happened?' Ryan arrives, leaning over my shoulder and getting in the way just at a crucial moment. Emmentine fires Dazzling Lights but only deals a grazing wound, the next bird dodges Ilva's Piercing Beam, and Roghod's Thunderstorm spell is the only attack that hits.

'Phew,' says Jude.

'Ryan, move.'

'Three vultures at once. This is intense. Hey!' Ryan rubs his ribs where I elbowed him.

'I said, *move*.'

'I only want to watch.'

He backs off, but now I can hear Paul whistling in the kitchen as he beats a wooden spoon around inside a mixing bowl and I can't concentrate.

Emmentine slashes and Mal fires and Ilva of the Moon summons Bewitching Light. The birds swoop down, snapping at Emmentine.

'Come on, come on,' says Ryan.

Emmentine musters her magic and unleashes a violent roar. Fireballs pour from her mouth. With a screech and a *whoomph*, the birds tumble to the ground, defeated.

'YES!'

'YOU DID IT!'

'WOO!'

From the kitchen there's a crash and a swear word.

'Before you fight anything else,' Jude reaches over and hits pause, 'I'll craft some arrows for

Mal and weave more scrolls for Roghod. Tia Treekeeper can use her healing spell too.'

While Jude crafts, Paul appears in the living room doorway.

'Why were you all shouting?' His apron is splattered with cake batter. 'I was making a cake, but now I'm not.'

'Why?' I ask.

'Because it's Saturday,' he says, which isn't a sensible answer.

Tia showers the party with a healing spell.

'We're about to fight the Mulch Queen,' explains Ryan.

'And a giant toad too,' says Jude.

'Toads are really vulnerable to being confused,' says Ryan. 'The only trouble is when they're confused they sometimes step on you.'

I catch the look Paul gives Ryan. Paul's eyebrows are right up and his forehead wrinkles.

'You're enjoying Illusory Isles then, Ryan?' Paul asks.

'What?' Ryan's voice is harsh.

'You just seem to know a lot about it.' Paul shrugs. 'I think that's pretty cool.'

'Well.' Ryan pauses as if he's working out

a retort. 'Yeah. Emmy needs me to dispense nuggets of big-brotherly wisdom sometimes.'

Paul's mouth twitches, but he doesn't actually laugh. Which is a shame, because Ryan was definitely making a joke.

Jude hands over the keyboard. 'Ready.'

My stomach twists up tight. This is only going to get harder.

'Right.' My fingers are sweaty. I unpause.

The toad stomps forward and the ground shakes. It opens its giant, sagging mouth—

Half the heroes run one way, half the other. Mal shoots and Emmentine swipes. Roghod chants a scroll spell. Before Ilva can cast an enchantment, a tide of swampish slime pours from the toad's mouth.

'Urgh.'

'Grim.'

It washes over Ilva's legs and she's stuck fast. The toad plods towards her. Any second it'll smash Ilva to bits.

'Uh oh.'

'Oh no.'

'Emmy, your heroes are going to die.'

'What are you lot groaning about?' asks

Mum, behind us. Mal shoots a flaming arrow and Emmentine swipes at the toad's side, but it's not enough. 'Paul, did you know there's broken crockery and cake mix all over the kitchen?'

'Shhh, Emmy's in the middle of something,' says Paul.

'Use the Spell of a Thousand Voices,' says Jude. 'I just made it.'

I tap as fast as I can. Roghod speaks and a thousand dizzying chants swirl around the arena. The toad sways for a moment and then heads in another direction, just as Ilva gets free. She sings Whispers of Midnight, and the toad roars in agony. A barbed arrow hits. A slash lands. The toad swipes and stomps, but it's not hitting anyone. Tia gets in a lucky hit with her knife and the toad keels over.

'Yeah!'

'Nice tactics, Ryan.'

Behind me, everyone celebrates, but I don't have time. The Mulch Queen descends from her throne and towers over the heroes.

```
Mulch Queen: You might defeat my beasts,
but you'll never be powerful enough to beat
my spell!
```

Then we battle.

This is what I'm good at. Emmentine dodges, swipes, dodges again as the Mulch Queen whirls round like a fist tornado. While Emmentine sprays fire, the other heroes run to the spell crystals.

POW. The Mulch Queen's fist comes from nowhere.

'Oooooh,' says Jude, as Emmentine goes flying.

'Ouch,' says Paul.

'Unlucky,' Ryan agrees.

Emmentine scrambles to her feet. I hit the roar combo and a fireball shoots from her mouth. It smashes into the Mulch Queen's side and she starts to smoulder. The companions dash around the arena clutching spell crystals. Emmentine sprints up to the Mulch Queen to swipe with her blazing claws. I aim and miss.

'Noooo.'

'Close one.'

'Come on, Emmy.'

The Mulch Queen belches poison fog, and Emmentine's health leaks away. But Emmentine still has one attack she hasn't used.

She chants a few words and out blasts a Cone

of Repulsing Flame. The Mulch Queen writhes and flails. This is her moment of weakness.

One by one, the companions slot their spell crystals into a new arrangement. The air fills with roaring and the Mulch Queen fills with light.

With a flash, she turns to stone—a great, ugly Mulch Queen statue.

Vines climb all over the Mulch Queen's stone features. They burst into bright blooms, flinging petals and seeds around the arena like confetti. Wherever the seeds land, they start growing.

'You did it!'

'You beat her!'

'Go, Emmentine, go.'

Paul shakes his fists in the air. Ryan punches me, in a nice way, I think. Even Mum applauds.

'We did it.' I can't stop grinning. 'We actually did it!'

'Paul, would you clear the cake batter up now?' says Mum.

'I'll clean it up and make another cake. A celebration for Emmy's victory.'

'Not just me, everyone helped.'

I high five Ryan then Jude with both hands.

On the screen, a cut-scene shows the mulch sliding off the Illusory Isles, and all the creatures shaking off their evil forms and becoming colourful and good once more.

'See? It was totally worth videoing,' says Jude. 'Shame it's too late to submit that to the Islandr tour. What was your Islandr video about, in the end?'

'Er …' I look at Ryan, who looks back at me blankly. 'Oh, that. I didn't actually make it.' Jude's eyes go wide. 'It took ages to find all the companions, and then I didn't have time to make a video as well,' I say, which is sort of true actually.

'Why didn't you tell me?' Jude asks.

'I thought you'd be annoyed after you helped me.'

Jude gives an exasperated sigh. 'Obviously not. I already know you're good, I don't need to see a video.'

'Yeah, Emmy,' says Ryan, 'maybe just believing in your friends is enough. Maybe you don't need outside proof.'

He's talking about the writing competition. I'm weighing up whether to shove him onto the sofa or knee his stomach when Mum shouts,

'Who wants to help make icing?' and before I can
do anything, Ryan's running for the kitchen.

IslandrChat

EMMENTINE
LOOK! I DID IT! *mulchqueensmash.mp4*
(im not going to put it on my channel because it has loads
of mistakes but im JUST SO EXCITED)

MeowMeow
OMG SPOILERS!!!

IndigoChalice
Woo! Go Emmentine!
Also I am *not* watching that video until I've defeated the
Mulch Queen myself thanks very much.

Emmentine
JadeMage helped. He made loads of cool potions and spells
and stuff. I never would of thought to do it myself.

LEVEL UP:
BOSS

TWENTY-
FIVE

On the morning of the summer fayre, I wake with
a jump in my stomach, like something important
is going to happen. Then I remember: the writing
competition results will be announced today.

Jude has to win the writing competition. He just
has to.

Mum's feet thud on the landing, as she hurtles
down the stairs. 'Get up, get up! Stallholders have
to be there by nine.'

But I'm awake already, dressed, and zipping up
my jacket. I squash my feet into my trainers and
follow Mum downstairs.

'Ryan!' Mum bangs on Ryan's bedroom door.
'Up!' *Bang.* 'Now!' *Bang.* 'Summer fayre!' *Bang,
bang, bang.*

'I'm not coming,' Ryan groans from inside.

'It's part of our deal—oh, Emmy. You look
incredible.'

I grin. The orange and gold sparks sewn on my
jacket wrap me up in fire. The gems crusted on my
trainers sparkle and flash.

'What does Emmy look like?' Ryan pulls open
his bedroom door. His eyes are bleary, his pyjamas
rumpled.

'Ryan,' says Mum, meaning business. 'Dressed
and out the house in ten minutes, or I take your
phone away for the whole summer.'

'You can't do that.' Ryan screws his face up. 'It's
human rights.'

'I'm your mother, I can do whatever I like. This
is your chance to help.'

Ryan slams the door. Mum shakes her head. 'He
was almost human yesterday. What happened?'

Ten minutes tick by as Paul, Mum, and me load
everything into our tiny car. Paul has never helped
us with the summer fayre before, so I have to keep
reminding him of everything we need to bring.

Mum marches to Ryan's door and knocks again.

'Phone,' she says.

'I'm coming.'

Ryan slinks out of his room, just about dressed,
in yesterday's chocolate-cake-stained T-shirt.
He flings himself on the car's backseat, his legs

squashed behind a bulging bag of cotton wool.

Then we're off.

We drive through the drizzle and arrive at school an hour before the fayre opens. Because we have a stall, we get to drive right onto the field to unload. I kneel up to stare through the windows.

In the mist, the rows of colourful tents and marquees look like a scene from Illusory Isles. I want to buy potions and meet companions and battle Mulchbeasts.

'If we set up quick, I can wrangle coffee from the PTA lady before the crowds come,' says Mum.

Paul grabs the face-painting chair. I pick up the board of face paint designs, modelled by six-year-old me.

'Ryan?' says Mum. 'Are you helping?' Ryan grunts. He sits in the car tapping his phone. 'Ug. Ryan. Big strong arms. Ug. Use arms help. Ug, ug.' Mum waves her arms like a dancing caveman.

'Why should I? It's not like you'll notice.' Ryan slams the car door shut.

Mum rolls her eyes at Paul. Paul sighs. I tape the laminated sign I made to the trestle table.

Temporary tattoos £1
Full face paint £2

It's not long before families are queuing at the school gates. The drizzle has disappeared and left the grass glittering. Drops still cling to my jacket and I brush them away.

I can't believe I'm going to wear my fiery jacket in front of school people.

'Emmy, we'll hold the fort if you want to look around,' says Mum. She hands me a jumble of coins.

I tuck my coins in my pocket and start walking, but my stomach feels tight. This is it. Soon actual people from my actual class will arrive, and they'll be able to see me, in my flaming jacket and my volcanic shoes.

'Emmy, over here!' Jude waves from a stall the next row over. He's standing beneath a sign that reads NAIL ART in glittery pink and purple. 'You're wearing them!' He points at my trainers.

'Of course!' I do a little dance to show them off.

'I painted Emmy's trainers, Mum,' he boasts to Sonja.

'Glittery shoes. I love it.' Sonja is lounging

in a garden chair. Today her hair is twisted in an elaborate knot above her head. 'You want your nails painted, Emmy? Only 50p.'

Last time Sonja asked me I didn't know what to say, but this time I'm going to be brave. 'Can you make my nails match my jacket?'

'That would be epic,' says Jude.

'Of course,' says Sonja. 'Put your hands flat on the table.' I sit, while she picks out orange, yellow, and red polish. 'You're my first customer, seeing as Jude refused.'

Jude crouches to stare at my trainers. 'The flames look really real. Mum, can I decorate my trainers too?'

'Not your new ones,' she says, wiping red drips off the nail varnish brush, 'they cost too much.'

'You look like an actual game character,' Jude says, and suddenly I feel like one, like I'm a fire elemental with magma claws.

'And did you notice the fayre looks just like the Mystic Market on Illusory Isles?' I say.

'Oh yeah!' Jude turns in a circle to look. 'There's probably Mulchbeasts lurking all over the place waiting to attack innocent children.' He points at the man on the sweet stall opposite, who is very short and has hair growing out of his nose instead of his head. 'Like him. I bet he's an evil goblin.'

'Not nice, Jude,' says Sonja. 'Emmy, you're all done. Careful not to smudge them. Jude, you sure you don't want your nails done too?'

'Can I just have one finger painted silver?' he asks. 'This will be my magic mulch-vaporizing finger'

'Let's go and investigate the goblin,' I say.

We buy mulchy snot worms (fizzy snakes), and chew their rubbery bodies as we walk away.

'Definitely a Mulch spy,' says Jude. 'Let's see if there are more.'

We push through crowds in summery clothes and flip-flops and run through a cloud of warm-dough-smell from the deep-fried doughnut van. We turn the corner and find ourselves back at Mum's face-painting stall.

'Here's trouble,' says Paul. He's squeezing a wet ball of cotton wool on the back of a tattoo for Harvey from Geek Gang. Mum is painting a bright orange tiger on Semira's face. Ryan is still in the car, eating his way through our snack supply.

'Emmentine!' says Harvey when he sees me. 'What's on your jacket?'

I spin in a circle to show it off. 'Jude decorated my trainers, too.' I lift my foot as high as I can. Jude grins.

'Is that Emmentine?' says Semira, opening her eyes just as Mum is trying to paint them. Mum smudges the paint and just manages to stop herself swearing.

'You need to hold still,' Mum says. 'Who's Emmentine?'

'I am.'

'It's her gaming name,' Jude explains. 'Like I'm JadeMage.'

'Are you Emmentine's mum?' asks Semira. 'Have you seen her video? Do you think she'll become a professional gamer?'

Mum ignores her. 'Just hold still so I can finish off your tiger stripes.'

'They're going to announce the results of the writing competition soon, aren't they?' says Harvey.

'Right after street dance,' says Semira. 'I can't wait, can you? I haven't seen Jemima Crown yet.'

'Vanessa says she's won, anyway,' Jude says.

'What?' Semira opens her eyes wide and her jaw hangs open. Mum sighs and gives up.

'Alright, Semira. You're done.'

'How would she know?' Semira says. 'She's just making it up.'

Jude shrugs. 'Apparently, she's going to be published.'

'I don't believe it.' Semira shakes her head. That makes me feel better. And anyway, I know for a definite fact that Jude's story is better than Vanessa's.

'Have you seen what's going on onstage?' asks Paul, pointing. 'There's some very, er, interesting dancing on at the moment.'

We follow his finger. The street dancers wiggle themselves into a V-shape, Vanessa in the middle, Lila and Ria further back, hands on hips.

'The mulch,' I hiss.

'Those accursed fiends,' Jude mutters. 'Little do they know that I will defeat them with my magic finger.' He flourishes his right hand and cackles.

'And I'll use my fire powers to set them on fire,' I say.

Jude stalks towards the stage, swishing an imaginary enchanter's cloak behind him, and I fire-stomp after him.

TWENTY-SIX

Thumping music blasts from the sound system. The dancers onstage zig and zag and stomp and point. Vanessa's long ponytail whirls around with every head toss.

'Zappapoof!' says Jude, pointing his magic finger at her. 'Zaggerblast!'

Vanessa whips her head round again and smacks Lila in the face with her ponytail. Lila flings her fingers and toes extra hard, keeping in perfect time, but Vanessa loses the beat and around her the other dancers do too.

'It's working!' I say. 'Keep going.'

Jude points and more nonsense spews from his mouth. 'Zigglyzoom! Zabracadabrah!'

Vanessa smiles a smug smile and stamps on Lila's toe, like it's part of the routine. Only Ria gives it away, by laughing so hard she can't keep up with the moves. The dance is falling apart.

Ella-May appears beside us with a big stick of candyfloss. 'They're rubbish, aren't they?'

'That's my fault,' says Jude, though he doesn't sound sorry about it. 'I've put curses on them.'

'Maybe I'll write a review for my blog,' says Ella-May. '*Three ways not to run a dance show.*' She tears off a hunk of candyfloss and it dematerializes into her mouth.

I smirk. 'I'd love to read that.'

'Where did you get that?' Jude points at Ella-May's candyfloss. 'Emmy, if we get a sugar cloud wand, we can cast an unmulchify shockwave across the whole school.' Ella-May points to the stall behind her. Jude turns to look at the line for the candyfloss stand, stretching nearly halfway across the field.

We can't go and stand in a queue like that! They're going to announce the competition results any minute.

Jude sees the queue and sighs, 'Maybe later then.' I let out a big breath.

Onstage, the music thumps to a triumphant end. Vanessa whirls to a stop, her teeth bared. Lila flings her arms out in a dramatic final freeze. Ria trips and nearly flies off the stage. A few people clap. As the dancers run offstage, the school caretaker carries on a table and three chairs.

'They're going to announce the results,' says Ella-May. 'See you after. Good luck!'

And before I can tell her that I haven't entered, she's gone, shouldering her way to the front of the crowd.

'Can we watch the results?' I ask Jude. Before he can answer, Lila bounds up to us. She's still in her green dancing tracksuit with a glittery star design on her cheek that looks like one of Mum's.

'You didn't watch the dance, did you?' she asks. We nod. Lila groans. 'It was awful. Vanessa took over all the choreography during rehearsals, and then she didn't even stick to it.'

'But you were really good,' I tell her. 'You stayed focussed, even when Vanessa was trying to elbow you.'

Lila stares into the distance, and the twist of her mouth shows she's thinking angry thoughts. 'Vanessa told me not to enter the writing competition, so I did. I don't think I'll win though. What about you?'

Something jabs into my back and I stumble. 'I didn't enter,' I say quickly. I get jabbed again, harder, and I spin around. It's Ria, leering, and Vanessa wearing a huge smirk.

'Oh my God, Emmy, you did hear what I said to Ria, didn't you? On Friday?'

I fold my arms to show her I'm not playing.

'Hear what?' says Lila, falling right into the trap.

'The winners already know we've won,' says Vanessa. 'They called us all into Mrs Trimble's office. I wasn't supposed to say anything, but then you went and eavesdropped when I was telling Ria.'

My insides dribble away into the trampled grass, but I stand totally still so Vanessa can't tell.

'Sorry, Emmy,' Vanessa says, as Ria stifles a giggle. 'I saw you put your entry in. But it's just a fact that I'm the best writer in the class. And you're … not.'

It's like she's stamping on my gooey remains. Job done, Vanessa drags Ria away, laughing.

I can almost feel Jude beside me, filling up with magic, ready to zap something.

'I thought you didn't enter,' he says.

'I honestly didn't. Vanessa's just saying that.'

'Then why—'

'She's a liar.' But I gulp, because I'm the liar this time. Jude says nothing. Lila's giving us a weird look. We watch as Mrs Trimble carries several mysterious envelopes onstage and lays them on the table. Today her outfit is mostly purple.

Marcus arrives. Before I can say hi, he crouches to stare at my trainers. 'Did you decorate your shoes yourself?'

I swallow again. 'Jude did.' I try to smile at Jude, but he won't smile back.

Lila gasps. 'Wow. Where did you get them?'

She stares at my Emmy-disease ridden trainers and doesn't even realize they're the same pair.

Marcus fishes in his pocket. 'Did Jude paint this as well?' And he pulls the Archmage of Ceren, with its purple cloak and teeny-tiny frown lines.

My eyes go wide. I stare at the plastic Warsorcery model. Jude stares at me. His chin starts to wobble.

Then he snatches the model from Marcus and stomps off.

Marcus opens and closes his empty hand. Lila gives me a look like, what is going on?

But I don't stop to explain. I'm chasing after Jude. Behind me, the sound system buzzes. 'It's my pleasure to introduce Jemima Crown, renowned children's writer, of *Supersonic Girl* and other superhero stories,' says Mrs Trimble's magnified voice. Ahead, Jude shoves between two dads with pushchairs, plunges through a gaggle of toddlers, and nearly smacks into Omar, before swerving round him. I elbow a teacher and barely have time to say sorry. Jude's getting away!

Then the crowd bursts into applause. The noise fills my head. 'Hello, Springhill School!' says a new voice to cheers and whoops.

I spot Jude's trainer vanishing through a crowd of noisy kids towards the meandering candyfloss queue. As the crowd gets thinner, I slalom around several mums in flowery dresses. Ahead, Jude starts to sprint.

Now Jemima Crown is going on about stories transporting you to other worlds. I wish I could open a door in this field and run to the Illusory Isles and take Jude with me. Then he would forget about all this. On the Illusory Isles, I could blast his mulchiness away and we'd be friends.

Jude pelts over the grass and I pelt after him, and my heart pounds and my legs slam and every gasp of breath feels like it has the power to make

Jude stay my friend for one more second.

'And now, I have the pleasurable task of revealing the overall winner of the Springhill story writing competition.' Jemima Crown's voice buzzes and crackles. 'The best story, as chosen by me, will be published in a real-life anthology of exceptional stories.' The audience mutters and squeals. 'So, without further ado . . .'

Jude reaches the candyfloss line and stops abruptly. I skid up beside him but he presses so close to the lady in front that his nose practically touches the back of her T-shirt.

'The winner is . . .' Jemima Crown leaves a big pause.

'Jude,' I pant, but he turns his face away, clutching the Archmage of Ceren in his fist. 'Jude!' I reach out to grab his arm, but he twists away.

'Ella-May Duffy!' shouts Jemima Crown. The crowd cheers. The lady in front of Jude claps politely.

I stare at the back of Jude's trembling head. After all that, he didn't win.

TWENTY-SEVEN

Ella-May from Geek Gang climbs onto the stage. Her shoulders are hunched and her face is red, but she's grinning.

In front of me, Jude counts his money for candyfloss. He still won't look at me.

At least Vanessa didn't win. Somehow, I don't feel as happy as I thought I would.

'Jude?' I try again.

On the stage, Jemima Crown lists all the wonderful prizes Ella-May's won. Jemima doesn't look anything like I imagined her. She's nearly as old as Mrs Trimble with short red hair and a dress that makes her look like an orange. I expected Vanessa's hero to be more glamorous. Jemima hands Ella-May one of the mysterious envelopes, but there are still two envelopes on the table.

'Jude!'

'What?'

I'm not expecting him to turn around, so when he does I say the first thing I think of.

'I gave it to Marcus when we fell out. The model, I mean. Anyway, I wouldn't have given it to him if you hadn't let Vanessa chase me into the toilets in the first place.'

It's not the right thing to say.

'If you're not buying candyfloss, just go away.' Jude's eyes are stormy and his cheeks puffy.

'Well, I am buying candyfloss. So there.' I fish out the coins in my jacket pocket. Only thirty pence left. Not even enough to buy the cheapest thing.

'I now have the pleasure of announcing the two runners-up,' says Jemima Crown. 'From our younger writers, Salma Ibrahim! And from our older writers, Jude Thomas!'

I stare. The ground rumbles a little, as if flowers will burst from the mulch any second. Jude hasn't even turned around.

'Jude,' I hiss, 'it's you.'

'Go away.'

'Jude Thomas?' says Jemima again. As Jude hears his name, his eyelids peel up and his mouth stretches down.

'Is Jude Thomas here?'

The crowd mumbles and mutters. They say Jude's name again and again and again.

'Is that you, dear?' asks the lady in front. 'Go on, you need to collect your prize.'

Jude's mouth snaps shuts. 'I didn't enter.'

'No, I entered for you.' He glares at me. 'Because you said you weren't going to, but I found your story in your bedroom and it was amazing and I thought you would win. And you did, see? Well, runner-up anyway, and you beat Vanessa which is practically winning.'

Now Marcus and Lila run towards us, waving and shouting Jude's name. Jude gives me one last glare and stomps towards the stage. I hurry behind.

'Ah, is that Jude?' says Jemima. Marcus marches in front shouting, 'Make way!' Lila skips beside Jude, singing, 'You did it, you did it, you actually did it!'

Now Jude's fists are clenched.

When I catch up, Lila whispers, 'What's up with Jude? Why isn't he happy?'

I don't know how to explain everything, so I say, 'It's my fault.'

When Jude gets to the stage steps, he stops.

Marcus pushes him, but he doesn't budge. He stares at Jemima and folds his arms.

'I didn't enter.' He says it like someone whose sums have been marked wrong when they're right.

'The Spell of Happiness?' Jemima asks, holding up the final envelope. 'About how an enchanter and an elemental undo a spell that makes everyone unnaturally happy?'

Jude nods. 'But I didn't enter it.'

'Well, now.' Mrs Trimble leans down and her jangly necklace swings near Jude's face. 'How did Ms Crown get hold of it if you didn't enter it? Come on, Jude. You've won a lovely prize.'

Mrs Trimble isn't the sort of person you argue with. Huffing, Jude climbs onto the stage.

Jemima Crown holds out her hand for Jude to shake, but Jude snatches his envelope and stands at the back of the stage. Jemima smiles at the audience, as if Jude is acting completely normally. 'Jude's wonderful story blew me away with its creative use of language. One to watch, Mrs Trimble.'

Jude rips his envelope open. He tips out the contents: a certificate and some fluttery pieces of card and two typed sheets—Jude's story.

'Let's give a big hand to our three wonderful writers,' says Mrs Trimble. The audience claps. Lila and Marcus cheer. Miss Monday's hands move so fast they look like they might fly off. I don't know whether I should be cheering or not.

Behind us, there's a shriek.

'Move, Ria!'

'I only asked—'

'Well, I'm going to fix it, OK? Get out my way.'

Elbowing her way through the crowd, all arms and lime green tracksuit and rage, is Vanessa. She hurtles towards the stage and leaps up, landing with a thump on her knees.

'This is ridiculous!' Her face is screwed up and red. 'How can you possibly make Jude a runner-up when I haven't won a single thing?'

Jemima's eyes go wide. She turns to Mrs Trimble for help.

'Come on, now, off the stage.'

'This competition was rigged,' Vanessa screams, but Mrs Trimble puts a hand on Vanessa's shoulder and steers her offstage.

'Let's have a calm discussion, shall we?' Mrs Trimble leads Vanessa to a quiet spot. Miss Monday rushes over and they both speak sternly to

Vanessa. After a moment, Vanessa gives them one of those fake smiles she's so good at. She waves a hand vaguely and walks away into the chattering crowd.

Jude and Ella-May step down onto the squelchy grass. Semira bounces over to Ella-May, cheering.

'That was epic,' says Marcus. 'Two winners from Geek Gang. Jude, can I read your story? Is it about Illusory Isles?'

But Jude pushes past him and marches over to me. 'Where are the pages you took from my room?' He waves his envelope in my face. 'They're not in here.'

'They're at home.' In the desk, where I hid them yesterday.

'Well, I want them back.'

'You'll get them back, I promise.' My eyes prickle. Everything good about today has gone wrong. I just want Jude to understand, but I don't know how to make him. 'You needed to win. You needed to realize you're good at something and you don't have to be jealous.'

'No, I just needed you to be a good friend.'

Marcus and Lila look at each other uneasily. Then Lila asks, 'What prize did you get?'

Before Jude can answer, his envelope is snatched from his hand.

'I wonder what's in here.' It's Vanessa. Her face is ugly with rage, and her hair half-falls from its ponytail. Ria's with her, but now she looks worried. 'Ooh, a certificate.' Vanessa pulls out the gold-edged paper.

'Give that back,' Jude whispers, holding out his hand for the envelope. I can tell he's going to cry.

Vanessa's mouth twists into a sneer. 'I'm still looking.'

I wait for Marcus or Lila to say something, but they stand as still and silent as if Vanessa has cast a spell.

Vanessa feels around inside the envelope. 'A *Supersonic Girl* bookmark, signed by Jemima Crown? I'll have that.' She pockets it. 'After all, I'm her biggest fan. Oh, and a gift card. Only twenty-five pounds. Obviously, she didn't like your story that much.'

That goes in her pocket too.

'But they're mine,' whispers Jude, while I think about how twenty-five pounds is enough to buy Illusory Isles and have enough left over for chocolate for Mum and pork pies for Paul.

'You don't actually deserve them though. Do you, Jude?'

Why doesn't Lila stand up to her? Marcus cares about things being done right, why isn't he doing the right thing now?

'Aren't you going to answer me?' Vanessa taps her foot. She's pulling the same trick she pulls with me. Questions with no right answers. My insides squirm like Mulchmaggots. I entered Jude's story into the competition. I made this happen. 'I'm just asking a question, Jude. There's nothing wrong with asking questions.'

I remember striding fast across the playground with Vanessa right behind me when she said the exact same thing. *It's just a question. What's wrong with asking questions?* I remember shouting for Jude and him running away. I remember standing in the toilets knowing it was pointless to fight back and hating Jude for not standing up for me.

The colourful, bustling fayre seems suddenly swamped in sluggish grey. Vanessa's going to win, just like she always wins. And this time I'm going to lose Jude for good.

'You don't deserve to win, do you, Jude? Do you?'

Jude shakes. A tear slides to the end of his nose and drips onto his shoe. He blinks. And then his eyes move, and just for a moment he looks right at me.

Maybe Vanessa doesn't have to win this time. Maybe I can do something. And even though it's Vanessa, and even though it probably won't work, I have to try.

I step in front of Jude. 'Leave him alone.'

'Or you'll what?' Vanessa rounds on me, snarling. I nearly step back, but I make myself stay.

'Give Jude his stuff back and go away. He won, not you, so get over it.'

'How cute. Jude, is Emmy your proper girlfriend now? How did that song go, Ria? The one you made up?'

'Er . . .' Ria definitely doesn't want to be here any more.

'Oh yeah, *Jude and Emmy kissing in a tree, ugly as two freaks can be.*' Vanessa cackles. My face is on fire.

'We're friends,' I say, but she just keeps laughing.

'And they're not freaks,' says Lila.

'Give the envelope back, Vanessa,' adds Marcus.

'Ooh, what's this?' asks Vanessa, and she pulls out Jude's story from the envelope. 'The Spell of Happiness. I can't wait to read this.'

'Give—' says Jude, reaching out, but Vanessa jerks it away.

'*On the island of mists and mountains, near the lake of crystal water, lived a hero known as JadeMage.* JadeMage?' Vanessa smirked. 'I suppose that's you.'

'Give!'

'*The wise mage, who was sage and learned, was preparing peace potions in his study . . .* I think sage is a type of herb, Jude.' It also means intelligent. Ryan told me that. My palms sweat and my heart thumps. This isn't working.

'But the Jade Mage would not leave without Emmentine the Brave, for she was the fearsomest fighter in all the land ...' Vanessa continues, but I'm only half listening now because I've remembered something.

Yesterday, when Emmentine beat the Mulch Queen, she could only do it with the help of her companions. That's what we have to do now.

'Marcus,' I hiss, 'we need help. As many people as you can find.'

'Geek Gang?'

252

'Exactly.'

He nods and runs into the crowd.

Jude tries to snatch his story from Vanessa.

'Let go!' shouts Jude.

'Or you'll what?' Vanessa snarls, gripping the edge of the pages. Any second they're going to tear.

Harvey and Omar run over, just as Vanessa yanks the story from Jude's hands.

'Leave him alone,' says Harvey.

'Give his story back,' adds Omar.

'Why?' says Vanessa. 'It was rubbish. Anyone could tell that Jude only won because Jemima felt sorry for him.' She yanks the pages from Jude's hand and he stumbles.

'Imagine if you had won, and then someone tried to steal the prize from you,' says Lila. 'You're just jealous because you wanted to win.'

'Why would I be jealous of Jude?' said Vanessa. She crumples the story between her hands. 'Oops. Sorry.'

'Yeah, how would you like it if someone scrunched up a story you'd worked on for ages?' Ella-May has arrived. She doesn't say it in a threatening way, but somehow she sounds really scary.

'Oh, get lost, you complete—'

'You weren't about to be mean to my friend, were you?' says Semira.

Marcus pants towards me. 'That's everyone I could find.'

'That's brilliant,' I whisper.

'Now what?'

All eyes are on Vanessa. My head is full of all the times she insulted me or made me feel small or asked an impossible question. I remember how small and powerless I felt shut in the toilet. But I'm not powerless any more. Maybe this time we really can stop her.

'We show her that bullies don't win.'

The summer fayre seems to grow into a massive stone arena. The mums and dads are buzzing, hissing Mulchbeasts and Geek Gang are my companions—enchanters and healers, fair folk and fighters—and we're ready to take on the Mulch Queen.

'Why are you picking on Jude, anyway?' asks Marcus. 'It's not like he's done anything wrong.' The spell has started, like a vine encircling the Mulch Queen.

'It's possible for two people to be good at the same thing, you know,' Harvey adds.

'One person can't be best all the time,' says Omar. 'I'm almost *never* best.'

Vanessa's face is scrunched up just like the paper in her hand. Her cheeks are red and her eyes are narrow. The vines are tightening.

'Why would you pick on someone because they won?' asks Semira. 'When someone wins something, you're meant to be happy for them.'

'Yeah, I'm always happy for you when you do good stuff,' says Ria, and this is the best of all, a Mulchbeast has suddenly turned on its master. 'I even said I'd help you with your book cover.'

Vanessa glares at Ria, gearing up for a four-armed attack.

'You're supposed to be my *friend*, Ria.' Her voice is a shriek. Her powers are failing. 'Anyway, it wasn't even a *real* competition. Anyone could tell it was rigged.'

'You always have to be the biggest and the best, but sometimes you're just not,' says Lila. The vines grip tighter.

'Lila,' Vanessa says, speaking in that pitying voice she always uses with me. 'Don't attack me just because we decided we weren't going to hang out with you any more. It's not our fault you're a toxic friend.'

She's regaining her powers. If I don't do something urgently, she'll destroy us all.

I walk right up to her, nose to nose. 'The only toxic person here is you. You act all nice, but you're a liar and you trick people into thinking you're cool. Well, you're not.'

'Exactly,' says Jude. It's the first thing he's said in ages. He lifts his head up and I can see glittering tear tracks, but he's not crying now. 'Vanessa, you're mean and you're a bully and none of us want to be like you.' The vines snap closed. The spell's complete.

Vanessa's chin trembles. Her eyes are liquid with rage.

She opens her palm and uncrinkles Jude's scrunched up story, stretching it out at each corner.

Then she tears it in two.

No one moves as it floats to the ground, as Vanessa stomps it into the dirt.

With a roar, Jude throws himself at Vanessa. Vanessa rams him back and he falls on me and together we tumble into the mud.

TWENTY-EIGHT

'You're both pathetic!' Vanessa screams. I try to breathe but I can't somehow, plus there's something knobbly digging into my stomach. 'You're small and stupid,' Vanessa rants. Jude groans and rolls off me and onto the smeared mud of the field. The knobbly thing is in his pocket. Vanessa's still going. 'You don't have any friends.' The Archmage of Ceren! That's where Jude put it when he snatched it from Marcus. 'Everyone would be better off if neither of you existed.'

I clutch my ribs and gasp and gasp. The air just won't go into my lungs.

Jude crouches next to me. 'Emmy?' He grabs my shoulder. I gasp.

'She's just doing it for attention, Jude,' Vanessa snarls, pulling him back by his T-shirt.

'Let go, Vanessa.'

'She's hurt!'

'Back off.'

Geek Gang stand over me. All I can see are shadows and legs. I heave another breath in, out, in. It's OK. I can nearly breathe properly again.

Jude reaches down to me. 'You stood up for me,' he says, as he pulls me to my feet.

'I had to,' I wheeze. 'We'll always look out for each other, remember?'

Vanessa lunges forward, but Ria grabs her arm. 'What?' says Vanessa, shaking her off. 'They deserve everything they get.'

'Miss Monday's coming,' Ria hisses.

Not just Miss Monday, but Mrs Trimble too, with Harvey and Omar trotting beside them.

'Vanessa tore up Jude's story,' says Harvey.

'And stole his gift token,' says Omar.

'And said all these horrible things.'

'We saw it all.'

Jude's story is still lying on the ground. I pick up the pieces, straighten them out, and wipe the mud off on my jeans.

'Vanessa Ferris.' Mrs Trimble's voice seems to shake the earth. Vanessa freezes. 'Show me what you've got in your pockets.'

Even now, Vanessa puts on a face like, *what, me?*

Mrs Trimble isn't fooled. 'Show me.'

Vanessa glares at Mrs Trimble's purple shoes as she pulls out the bookmark and throws it on the floor.

'Vanessa.'

'What?' Vanessa looks up a Mrs Trimble, but Mrs Trimble stares back. Around us, parents mutter or drag their toddlers away. Vanessa's big sister, in short shorts and a tiny top, walks over carrying two ice creams. When she sees Vanessa getting told off, she stops dead and rolls her eyes. Nearby, Jemima Crown is chatting to some teachers. When she sees what's happening, she turns to watch.

Vanessa bends to pick up the bookmark and hands it to Mrs Trimble. Then she pulls out the book token, lifts it as if to throw it on the floor too. I jerk forward. So does Jude, and half of Geek Gang. But at the last second, Vanessa hands it over.

'Mrs Trimble, I'm sorry to see the competition has caused an upset,' says Jemima, hurrying towards us. 'Does one of our winners need a new signed bookmark? Or, how about a copy of my new book?'

Vanessa shoots a look at Jemima. Then

something happens that I never expected. She bursts into noisy sobs. 'You've ruined everything,' she wails, though I don't know who she means.

'My office,' Mrs Trimble snaps. 'Now. You too, Jude. Who else was involved in this?'

We all raise our hands.

'Right, all of you.' With that, Mrs Trimble marches off across the field. Vanessa stomps after her, arms folded. Her sister turns away, taking alternate licks of both ice creams. Jude gives us all a wide-eyed look as we trail behind.

This is it. We're going into Mrs Trimble's office. Alien headquarters.

■ ■ ■ ■

I've never been in the head teacher's office before. People only go to the head teacher's office if they get ten out of ten on their spellings three weeks in a row, or get a star reader certificate, or earn their 100m swimming badge, or sometimes when they're in really big trouble, like now. So I've never been.

The office is very crowded with Mrs Trimble and Vanessa and half of Geek Gang crammed in, and to top it off, Jemima Crown stands in the doorway signing a copy of *Supersonic Girl* for Jude.

'Vanessa, I'm ashamed,' says Mrs Trimble.
Vanessa's face is pale and she stares in front of her
in an undead sort of way. 'I'm ashamed that a child
can join this school and think that they can behave
like that.'

Vanessa's chin wobbles. Good.

Mrs Trimble says she's going to talk to us one
by one to hear our side of the story. While we
wait outside, on the squashy seats in the corridor,
Jemima Crown hands Jude his brand new copy of
Supersonic Girl.

'Jude, you're a natural storyteller,' she says. 'I
know you said you didn't enter, but I'm glad I got
to read your story anyway.'

Then Mrs Trimble's door opens. 'Emmy, you
next.'

I breathe in deep and march inside.

'Sit down.' She points to the special star-shaped
stool you usually only get to sit on if you're a star
reader. 'Now, describe what happened between Jude
and Vanessa on the field,' she says, so I do.

'Why do you think Vanessa picked on Jude?'
Mrs Trimble asks next, so I tell her about Vanessa
being jealous of Jude and also hating me.

Then Mrs Trimble asks me what I mean by

'hate', so I tell her all about the time Vanessa followed me into the toilets. Mrs Trimble says, 'Why didn't you tell a teacher?' and I say, 'I already tried that, but it just made everything worse.' But the funny thing is, I'm not worried any more. I'm so not-worried that I'm swinging my legs and my hands are lying normally on my lap and not even fiddling with my T-shirt hem. I don't think Vanessa can hurt me, not now I have Geek Gang on my side.

When I leave the office, Jemima is collecting her bags to leave. Ella-May sits onto the squashy seats next to a sniffling Vanessa.

'Tell her, then,' Ella-May says.

'No, she hates me now,' says Vanessa. She's not crying any more but her face is blotchy.

'She won't hate you if you tell her you're her number one fan. Writers love to meet their number one fans.'

'Jemima Crown, wait!' says Vanessa, throwing herself in front of the door, so Jemima can't leave. 'I'm sorry about all this,' Vanessa gestures to us as if we were the ones making trouble, 'but the honest truth is, I've read all your books, some of them at least three times, and I really want to be a writer like you one day, so will you sign a bookmark for me?'

Jemima doesn't tell her off. In fact, she smiles and pulls a pen from her pocket. 'Of course! I'm so pleased to have met my number one fan at last.' Vanessa doesn't look nearly as miserable when she sits back down next to Ella-May to show off her bookmark.

Jude is nearly the last person to speak to Mrs Trimble except for Vanessa, but I wait with him the whole time. He's still in there when a woman arrives. She's wearing very smart clothes, but her hair is sticking to her face and her mascara is smudged.

'Vanessa!' she says. Vanessa sighs and looks in the other direction. 'Your sister just called me. I can't believe you've managed to get yourself into trouble at the school fayre. What's got into you?'

'It's this school!' Vanessa clenches her fists and her bookmark bends in the middle. 'I hate it. Everyone thinks I'm stupid or something.'

'We don't think any such thing.' Mrs Trimble stands in her office door, gazing at Vanessa. 'Now why don't you both come in and we'll have a chat, shall we? Off you go, Jude.'

Jude dashes towards me and we head back outside onto the field.

'Did you write the end of my story yourself?' he asks.

'Ryan helped. He gave me ideas for all the good descriptions.'

'It's not bad,' he says, holding out the typed pages, 'but I would have written it better. Also, you got one thing wrong.' He points to the very last paragraph, where JadeMage and Emmentine have a party to celebrate. 'They can't eat pizza, because there's no such thing as Italy in the Illusory Isles universe.'

Whoops. The pizza was my idea. 'What do they eat at parties, then?'

'Gingerbread and currant cakes and honey fritters,' Jude says. 'That's the sort of thing they ate in medieval times. It's OK though, I still got runner-up.' He smiles reassuringly at me.

Suddenly, Mum and Sonja swoop down on us.

'Where were you?' says Mum.

'We've been looking all over,' says Sonja.

'It wasn't that Vanessa girl again, was it?' asks Mum.

'It's fine,' I say, 'we vanquished her.'

'Jude, you got runner-up!' Sonja wraps Jude in a hug.

'Mum, what about the stall?' I ask.

'Never mind the stall,' says Mum. 'Paul can manage.'

'But he's never done the summer fayre before. What if someone wants their face painted? Or he forgets to keep an eye on the cash box and someone steals it?'

'Emmy.' Mum pulls a face. 'Who would steal anything at a school fayre?' She obviously doesn't know about kids.

'Come on.' I grab Mum's hand, drag her at volcano-shoe Megaspeed towards our stall.

When we reach it, the stall is lost in a huge crowd.

Ryan sits on the chair behind the table handing out temporary tattoos and damp cotton wool. 'One pound per tattoo,' he says, counting the money and throwing it into the cash tin. 'Did anyone order extra glitter?' That's when I spot the sign. On the bottom, in marker pen, it says:

Why not add GLITTER for only 50p?!

We were giving it away for free before!

'Ryan, someone for a robot,' says Paul. He's at the face-painting chair, where a small boy with his face painted like a ginger cat is just hopping down.

'Be right there,' says Ryan. He and Paul switch places. Ryan grabs the grey face paint and Paul hands out the next batch of tattoos.

'Paul, what's going on?' asks Mum.

'Ryan told me I wasn't running the stall right,' Paul explains. 'So I got him to show me how.'

'And then we made some innovations,' Ryan adds, painting green and yellow buttons on the girl now sitting on the tall chair. 'The only problem is that Paul can only paint animals and I can only paint knights and robots, so we have to keep swapping.'

'But—you—how?' Mum doesn't seem to be able to say a full sentence, but I know what she means. Paul mouths, 'later,' and winks.

'You can put your feet up for a bit, Mum,' Ryan offers.

Jude is gawping at the tattoos on people's arms as they leave. 'They're not real, are they?'

Mum laughs. 'You'd be lucky, for a quid.'

'Do you want to get one?' Jude asks me. 'We

could get matching ones.'

'Go on, Emmy,' says Ryan, handing us a few sheets to look at. 'That's what *friends* do.' He makes friends sound really significant.

But before we can pick, Marcus and Lila arrive. 'Jude, do you play Warsorcery then?' says Marcus. Him and Lila are both holding big ice creams, which dribble down the side of the cones.

'A bit.' Jude puts his hand in his pocket, the pocket with the Archmage. 'Don't get the chance, much.'

'Do you want to come over and play?' says Marcus. 'I have a gaming table at home.'

Jude's eyes go wide. 'That'd be great.'

'Emmy, do you remember that game we used to play?' Lila says. 'Where we were superheroes and we thought Mrs Trimble was an alien doing experiments on children?'

'Oh yeah,' I say as if I haven't thought about it for a long time.

'That was fun,' says Lila, and she licks an ice cream dribble from her hand. 'We should play it again.'

'We can if you want,' I say. 'Next week? Jude's good at playing it too.'

I join Jude where he's inspecting the different tattoo designs. 'I'm sorry I took your story. It's just, I thought you were jealous because I made a famous video and I wanted you to see that you can do stuff too.'

'I don't care about that,' says Jude. 'I thought you didn't want to be my friend any more. You were making all these new friends at Geek Gang and the only reason you hung out with me was because I had Illusory Isles II and you didn't, and then you got that too, and I just wanted you to keep being my friend.'

'Jude! *Obviously* you're still my friend. And Illusory Isles is more fun when we're playing together.'

Jude holds the Archmage of Ceren out. 'Do you want this back?'

'I definitely do! We'll always look out for each other, right?'

'We'll always look out for each other.' Jude grins and throws his arms around me in a big hug.

Lila and Marcus stare. I stand, my arms dangling, waiting for them to giggle or sing the Emmy and Jude kissing in a tree song. But no one does.

So I hug Jude back.

Islandr Message Boards

Video: OFFICAL Emmentine Highlights Reel

play video

IndigoChalice

It's the video you've all been waiting for – watch the amazing Emmentine play Illusory Isles II from the moment she steps onto the Isle of Shade to the final battle against the Mulch Queen! Will she be triumphant? Only one way to find out . . . xoxoxo

Comments

MeowMeow

EMMENTINE SURPRISE! We made a vido for you! (I hope you don't mind)

Emmentine

WHAT?!?!?!?!?!?!?!?!?! This is SO COOL.

JadeMage

I love the bit in the cave where you get completely destroyed by Mulchbats haha

TWENTY-
NINE

Bang!

'Paul?' Mum rests her paintbrush on the kitchen
table.

Smash!

'Ryan!' she shouts. She pokes tiny dots of black
paint into the eyes of the Warsorcery model she's
holding. I rest my elbows on the table to keep my
hands steady and poke in two black eye dots, just
the same. Jude gave me the models so that I can
play Warsorcery with him and Marcus.

From the front room comes an air-ripping fart
noise. Paul and Ryan laugh their heads off. Mum
thumps her plastic foot soldier on the table.

'First, we invite them to do an art project with
us and they're too busy, now they're interrupting
our peaceful painting time with their noise.'

'At least they're making noise *with* each other,
not *at* each other.'

Mum smiles. 'I know.' *BOOM!* 'Still, it's very loud.'

'Shall I ask them to turn it down a bit?'

'Would you?'

I lay my paintbrush on the newspaper so the end doesn't get bent, then pad to the living room.

Paul and Ryan are crammed at the computer, watching a video. As I come in, Emmentine skids across the screen, apparently powered by her farts, which explode into a series of fireballs, *whoomph, whoomph, whoomph*. Paul and Ryan cackle.

'The timing is spot on,' says Paul, in that squeaky voice people use when they're about to burst out laughing again.

'The way she—the way she—bunny-hops along—with each parp,' chokes Ryan.

I jump onto the sofa behind them. 'What are you doing to my videos, now?'

'You have to see this,' says Ryan. 'It has ten times as many farts as the last one.'

'And burps too,' adds Paul.

'Yeah, no need to boast about your burps. They sound more like an earwig clearing its throat.'

'Hey, who taught you how to sound edit?' But Paul is grinning. I think he's worked out not to take Ryan's big brother talk too seriously.

Paul scrolls to the beginning of the video. It starts off just like my latest Islandr video, with Emmentine and her companions surrounding the Mulch Queen in her stone fortress. As they reach the Mulch Queen, instead of cackling, she goes into slow-mo and emits a billowing cloud of green gas and a loud sound that's suspiciously like an earwig clearing its throat.

I can't help giggling. 'Is that meant to be realistic?'

'No, actually, it's meant to be ridiculous,' says Paul, all defensive. 'It's called comedy.'

'That's what he thinks,' says Ryan.

Paul and Ryan do this a lot, now: editing my videos to add more explosions and fart jokes. They posted their first one a few weeks ago and already it's got more hits than mine.

'Hey,' Mum pokes her head round the door. 'What are you lot doing? I thought you were going to turn the volume down.'

■ ■ ■ ■

The Warsorcery models are practically dry by the next morning, so I tuck them in my fire jacket pocket to take to school, before doing up the laces on my flame trainers. Miss Monday said my trainers were 'gorgeous, but a little outlandish to wear every day.' But today is special: it's the last day before the half term holiday.

Mum walks me to school. Even though it's one of those shivery mornings, she doesn't wear a jumper.

'Aren't you cold?' I ask, as her ink-purple arms go goosebumpy.

'It's summer!' She flings her arms out and shakes her hair which is now pale pink. The Rice Krispie cakes in the plastic box she's holding slide about. Paul made them for my class party. 'Sunshine, warm air, long days.' She whirls around, so I grab the box from her before the cakes get smashed. 'There's always more to look forward to in summer. Don't you feel it?'

There's lots I'm looking forward to, not just summer things, but hanging out with Jude, Lila and Marcus and learning to play Warsorcery.

But best of all, I don't have to worry about Vanessa any more. She hasn't tried anything since the summer fayre. Her parents had another long talk Mrs Trimble and Miss Monday, and she had to do her work in a separate room for a week. Ever since, we've had all these lessons about how it's OK to be different and what to do if we see someone getting picked on. I don't know if it will help, but it's a nice break from writing stories every day. Whenever we do have story-writing lessons, Miss Monday always gives Vanessa something extra hard to write. For some reason this seems to make Vanessa happy. Anyway, if she ever tries anything, now I've got lots of people to stand up for me, and that's why I think she won't bother.

So, I'm only a bit nervous walking into the classroom in my flame trainers and fire jacket. There's no need to worry, though.

'Fire stomp shoes!' shouts Jude as soon as he sees me. Jude wears a green T-shirt with an Illusory Isles enchanter on the front. 'Mum found it on the internet,' he says, stretching it down to show me. 'It's not as good as yours, but it'll do for now.'

'Warsorcery tonight?' Marcus asks. 'I've got some new horseback wizards I want to try out. They have all these wind spells.'

'Emmy's going to play too,' says Jude.

'I even brought my models, look.' I pull out the two foot soldiers from my pocket.

'They're so good,' gasps Marcus.

'Especially that one.' Jude points to the one Mum painted, but I don't tell him that.

Lila dives onto the carpet next to us. 'You're wearing your magic trainers!' she says. 'When are we going to do mine? You promised.' Ever since Lila found out my fire trainers are the same ones as her Emmy disease trainers, she's been begging us to decorate hers too. Jude said he would do the design and I said we could use Mum's pens and gem stones. 'I want them midnight blue with silver moons and gold stars. We have to do it soon.' Lila is quite forceful when she's not under Vanessa's spell.

'This weekend?'

'Yay!'

Vanessa sits on the carpet, a little way away from everyone else. These last few days I've seen her talking with Ella-May at break. Well, not talking. They sit next to each other on the same bench, each reading a Jemima Crown book, or scribbling in their notebooks. Lila says Vanessa really doesn't write any secrets in her notebook—

just stories.

'Are you ready,' says Miss Monday, sweeping into the classroom, 'for the most brilliant gaming video ever produced in the history of the Earth, directed, designed, and edited exclusively by the Geek Gang?'

'Yeah!' the class cheers. Miss Monday cheers too. She pulls the blinds shut and hits play.

Electronic music begins to beep and jiggle. The video title bursts onto the screen.

There's More Than One Way to be a Hero

The title fades. People whisper as Lila appears onscreen.

'My favourite game is Animal Hotel,' she says, as a video of Animal Hotel plays in the background. Omar added the special effects. In real life, Lila was just standing in front of the green screen.

'My superpower is designing new outfits for pets,' says Lila. 'I design the outfits on my computer and then other players download them for their dogs and cats to wear.'

Next up, Marcus talks about Underfleet.

'My superpower is tactics,' says Marcus. Behind him, an army defends a stone keep. 'In this case, the archers defend the castle, shooting over the heads of the infantry, while three battalions attack from three directions. The enemy doesn't stand a chance.'

Then Jude appears. 'My superpower is crafting items, especially potions,' says Jude on the video.

Real-life Jude buries his head in his hands. 'It's too embarrassing,' he whispers. Screen Jude explains how to make the most devastating spell potions, but real Jude doesn't look up once.

Finally, it's me. My cheeks go warm and I try and squash a goofy grin. On the video, I shuffle my legs one way then the other. I wish I'd stood still.

'My superpower is my skill at beating the baddies,' says video me. 'I level up my character and find the best companions. Then when it's time for the fight, I'm totally prepared.' A clip plays from the final battle against the Mulch Queen. Emmentine runs, swipes, roars. The Mulch Queen explodes in a cloud of greenery.

Vanessa leans forward.

'And that's how you defeat the Mulch Queen,' says video me. Vanessa's mouth hangs open. She doesn't realize I'm sort of, a little bit, talking about her.

'As you can see,' says video Semira, 'everyone has

a superpower. What's yours?'

The beepy background music bounces to an end and the credits roll.

The class bursts into applause.

'I hope you all enjoyed that,' says Miss Monday. 'Geek Gang will be continuing after the holiday, and our new project will be . . .' she pauses, and everyone drums their hands on their knees to create a drum roll, '. . . blogging! So if you're a budding writer or you've got something you want to geek out about, come along.'

Vanessa's hand shoots up, but she doesn't wait to be picked. She hasn't completely changed. 'Do you have to write about computer games?'

'No, just about something you really love. It could be games or music—'

'Or books?' Vanessa asks.

'Exactly,' says Miss Monday.

Jude gives me a wide-eyed look and Lila pulls a face like she can't believe Vanessa is going to spoil Geek Gang, when the whole point was to get away from her.

I shrug. I don't think it's possible for Vanessa to spoil Geek Gang now. After all, there isn't a single person in Geek Gang who doesn't know what she did at the summer fayre. She'll just have to make friends by being nice, like everyone else.

'By the way,' says Jude, as Miss Monday sends us off moving chairs and tables out of the way to make room for the class party, 'you got your superpower wrong.'

I frown. 'No, I didn't. I'm great at fighting.'

'On Illusory Isles you are.' Jude puts his plate of cheesy ham cubes skewered on cocktail sticks on the food table. I add Paul's Rice Krispie cakes, then I eat a cheesy ham cube quick, so that I definitely get one before they all go. 'But in real life, your best superpower is standing up for your friends,' Jude says.

I'm puffing up as I hide the cocktail stick in my fire jacket pocket. My trainers have Megaspeed. If Jude was in trouble, I could run to his side, *flash*, in a nanosecond. My jacket is a power-shield. If anyone tries to hurt my friends, *bam*, they're blasted to outer space.

Vanessa comes over to add a plate of pizza slices to the food table. Today she doesn't say a mean word or even give me a nasty look.

Perhaps she knows about my real-life superpowers too.

ABOUT HELEN HARVEY

Helen Harvey grew up in a wild and unruly corner of the internet, where she dodged flames, crafted websites, and led a guild of magical wolf-tamers. She completed the Bath Spa MA in Writing for Young People with Distinction and won the 2017 United Agents Prize. She lives in Bristol with her gaming partner and two furry writing companions. *Emmy Levels Up* is her first novel.

Twitter: @HellionHarvey
Website: www.helen-harvey.com

ACKNOWLEDGEMENTS

Huge thanks to my fabulous agent Lauren Gardner for believing in Emmy and fighting her corner. Enormous thanks to Liz Cross, who was first to ask for more. Mega thanks to Clare Whitston for being a fabulous editor, and to the team at Oxford Children's, including Hannah Penny, Rob Lowe, and everyone working behind the scenes. Thanks to Abbey Lossing for the gorgeous cover and to Liz Scott for her hard work.

This book started on the Bath Spa MA Writing for Young People and wouldn't exist without the wonderful tutors and students I met there. Massive thanks to Julia Green for a wonderful course, to Elen Caldecott for being the perfect tutor, to Janine Amos who gave the prompt that set Emmy off, and to Lucy Christopher and CJ Skuse who helped her level up. I would like to thank every person in the 2016/17 cohort by name, but that might take too many pages, so I'd particularly like to mention Elena Andersen, E Regina Byers, Max Boucherat, JM Briscoe and Rebecca Fishwick. You're all superheroes!

Thanks to the Scholars Walkers for advice, the Good Ship for cheerleading, and the Swaggers for gifs (you know which ones). Thanks to Beth Webb, Stacey, Tamsin, Heather and Chris, who I talked into reading early versions and giving me feedback. Mega thanks to Charlie for helping me think of titles.

Mum, thank you so much. Without your help I couldn't have done the MA, and without all those Kilve courses I might not be a writer.

Chris, endless thanks for supporting me when I quit my "proper job" to pursue a dream, for listening patiently during one-sided conversations about book plots, and for always noticing typos. You're my favourite.

Eternal chin scratches to Loki and Freya who brought me socks and reminded me when it was dinner time.

This is only the tip of an iceberg of people who made me a writer and who made this book possible. If I've missed you, I'm so sorry. Please add yourself here:

_____

You are very appreciated, and I couldn't have done this without you!